The Mc
Best wishes
Dawn Maith

Gap Year

by
Dawn I Maith

Strategic Book Publishing and Rights Co.

Strategic Book Publishing and Rights Company
12620 FM 1960, Suite A4-507
Houston TX 77665
www.sbpra.com

ISBN: 978-1-61897-214-9

Design: Dedicated Book Services, Inc. (www.netdbs.com)

For David, my inspiration and for Joy and Sian.
For their encouragement, their faith and their help.

Thank you.

She held the plastic wand in her hand. It was wet and she tilted it so as to avoid spilling urine on her fingers. No matter how long she looked at it the message was still the same. One word not two. Just one. Pregnant. Slowly she started to cry.

PART 1
WINTER

CHAPTER 1

He opened the door and called her name "Soph... you home?"

The lack of response didn't necessarily mean she was out, but he knew it was significant. He walked into the kitchen and saw straight away why she hadn't answered. She was sitting at the kitchen table and as he took in the tear-stained mascara-streaked face and the vodka bottle in front of her he knew this had been a bad day.

He placed a hand on her shoulder and went to kiss her cheek but she pre-empted him and turned away. She was totally wrecked; how long had she been sitting there drinking? He was home at the usual time and by rights she should only have been home about twenty minutes but this was the aftermath of several hours drinking. Sitting down next to her he took her hand and tried to make eye contact, when she refused he took her chin and drew her head up so they could look at each other. In response she closed her eyes to avoid his gaze.

Giving up he rose, moved the vodka bottle away from her onto the worktop and filled the kettle. "Coffee?... Tell you what I'll make it and you drink it if you want ok?"

"I need sobering up then do I? I'd rather stay pissed if it's all the same to you thanks."

"I don't care if you're pissed or not I want a coffee and you can suit yourself but I'd like to know why you're pissed at six fifteen on a Tuesday evening."

"Would you really?"

"Soph, whatever it is of course I want to know. You're clearly really upset and I want to help," his voice softened as he knelt in front of her.

"Is it what I think? Did you come on?" She laughed bitterly.

"I'm so fucking predictable aren't I? I'm crying so it must be my period. Actually you're right; I'm not pregnant this month, same as last month, same as every other month before. Well done Sherlock Holmes. That would have been bad enough but that little slag at work..."

"Kirsty?"

"Yes, that little tart is pregnant. She told us today." He sighed and took her hands in his. Kirsty worked in Sophie's office, he knew nothing about her except for the fact that her skirts were too short, her heels were too high, her perfume too strong and the male staff loved her, which meant Sophie hated her.

"Sweetheart, I am so, so, sorry, it's not our time that's all, it'll be us soon, I know it, come here." He attempted to put his arms round her but she resisted and he slowly began to realize there was more to this than just the crushing disappointment. He gave her a second and finally, between gut wrenching sobs she told him the rest.

"She only told us because she needs some time off, not because she's unwell, oh no, it's 'cause she's having an abortion. She isn't even ashamed she was so cold, so clinical and of course, no mention of the father. Bitch! That baby should have been ours not hers, what gives her the right to kill a baby when we want one so badly? It's just not fair. Why us? Why isn't it our turn?" She was sobbing so much she could hardly speak and she collapsed into his arms on the floor. He held her until the sobs abated and she lifted her head slowly to look at him.

"I'm sorry, Tom it's just so hard, she dropped the bombshell this morning and I came on at lunchtime. I had to come home, told them I was ill."

He stroked her hair and kissed her forehead. "It's ok, I feel as disappointed as you, that cow should keep her sodding mouth shut. Makes me so angry, people like that, tactless and thoughtless."

Sophie suddenly pushed away from him, her eyes blazing with fury. "What do you mean by that? You're only angry 'cause she told me not because she's killing a baby that should have been ours."

"That's not what I meant at all, I just thought she was tactless which added to your pain. Of course I'm furious that she's getting rid of a baby when you want one so badly…"

"*I* want one. Not *we* want one? It's just me then? You bastard you have no idea how I feel, you don't give a shit whether we have kids or not do you? Get away from me," she pushed him and he fell backwards.

"Sweetheart, it's not like that at all, I'm sorry I upset you," but she was already halfway up the stairs and within a matter of seconds he heard the bedroom door slam.

He stood up.

"Bollocks." Reaching for the vodka he took a hearty swig. He knew it was the alcohol and the hormones talking but this emotional roller-coaster was killing him. Every month it was the same; ovulation predictors, thermometers, charts, only certain positions were allowed, abstinence the rest of the month, when was the last time they'd made love without an agenda, come to think of it when was the last time they'd just fucked 'cause they felt horny. Jesus, it was months ago. Maybe he could just wank into a Tupperware box and stick it in the freezer with a note and a turkey-baster, she could help herself then. If she knew he had even the occasional wank she'd go mad. Another shot of vodka and he was feeling seriously pissed himself.

"Need to eat something, mate," he muttered. He settled for a ham sandwich, packet of crisps and some Jaffa Cakes. He knew Sophie wouldn't eat anything tonight; she never did when she was feeling like this, and hopefully she would sleep it off.

Before her biological alarm had gone off they would always have great sex after a row, rough, dirty and animalistic, now, sex was for having kids and not to be squandered on making their relationship better. 'Trying for a baby what a ridiculous phrase' he thought bitterly, 'trying's ok but failing is really hard work.'

* * *

Sophie slammed the bedroom door behind her and crumpled onto the floor. Huge sobs erupted from her as she held her head in her hands. The pain of this latest disappointment was so acute, so physical it felt truly unbearable. There was no answer, no solution, and no remedy. The GP had told them it was too soon for a referral and that they should relax and just try for another year and see what happened. Eight months in and nothing. Regular cycle, regular sex, the most favorable positions, etc, etc, etc. It was all shit. Sometimes she felt as if she was in this thing alone. Tom didn't care if they had kids; he said he would be happy either way, what did that mean for

Christ's sake? You want kids or you don't there's no middle ground. She stood up and made her way to the bathroom, turning on the shower she caught sight of herself in the mirror and was truly shocked. Her face was ghostly white, her eyes dark rimmed and bloodshot, her hair was a mess and her clothes were wrinkled and grubby. How could this be happening to her? She was always so much in control, well groomed, happy at work, lovely husband, nice home, good lifestyle. The only piece missing from the puzzle was a baby. Maybe this was the price for her great life? Maybe she'd had it too good for too long? Maybe God didn't want her to be a mum?

"Oh dear God, please no...not that," another small sob escaped her.

She shed her clothes and stepped into the hot water, instantly she felt better. They could try again next month. It was only a few weeks to wait. Her spirits began to rise until she saw the trickle of blood running down the inside of her thigh and the thought of Kirsty's abortion felled her to her knees.

* * *

When Tom heard the shower go off, he waited ten minutes and headed upstairs. He saw her in the half-light, her back to him feigning sleep. Silently he undressed and slid in next to her. Snuggling up to her he found himself strangely aroused. He'd noticed this had happening more and more recently, he figured it was just knowing he wasn't allowed to shag anytime made him want to. Rebelliously he pushed his erection against her, knowing sex was off the menu always made him worse.

"Back off, Tom" she growled.

"Sorry, thought you were asleep," he lied.

"Do you usually rub your hard-on all over my arse when I'm asleep then?"

"Gotta take what I can get these days, hun." She started to smile. This was always how they'd made up after rowing before all the fertility stuff started.

"We can't, you know that. I'm on for one and we have to abstain..."

"For Christ's sake why can't we just touch or kiss or mess around when we want? I love you and yet I can't touch you unless a bloody plastic stick smiles and says so. What's going on, don't you want to even touch me now?"

Rolling over Sophie's tone softened.

"Of course I do." She reached for him, "I would love to fool around with you right now but this is too important. What if we didn't get pregnant this month because of one blow-job?"

He groaned and began to move his hips so that his penis was moving in her hand. "Oy you, stop it." She let go.

"Shit, Soph can we please just act like a normal couple, just once, 'cause I don't think I can carry on like this without you and me getting back to basics now and again, I want to make love to my wife, is that too much to ask?"

She sighed, she wanted to say 'no' and take him in her hand and shut all the pressures of the world out but she just couldn't, she was so focused on her goal even his feelings didn't matter.

"Sophie....I want you," his hand went to her breast.

"No, Tom, no...I don't feel like it," she snapped. They were both angry now.

"Well I don't feel like it every time you're ovulating but I have to perform so why can't we just make an exception?" He took her nipple in his mouth and as she tried to pull away he pushed her on to her back.

"Tom, stop."

"Not this time, it's my turn to be a man not a fucking sperm donor." His hand pushed towards her pants and hooking them with his fingers he pulled them down.

"Tom, get off me."

"I told you no!" He was on top of her now and was forcing her thighs apart.

"Tom, for God's sake you're scaring me. Stop it." She was starting to cry but he had passed the point of no return.

Pushing his hand between her legs he fumbled for the tampon cord and pulled.

"Ow! No please stop it please." Sophie was scared and really crying now, the reality of how they had gone from an unwanted erection to this was unbelievable. Within seconds she felt him push into her and any illusion of arousal or escape evaporated. He came quickly and rolled off her immediately.

"Soph, I'm so sorry...I don't know what happened. I didn't mean to hurt you." He held her but she lay staring at the ceiling with tears falling from her eyes onto the pillow.

"Soph...Soph."

For the second time that night Sophie showered and Tom reached for the vodka.

* * *

Tom's phone alarm went off and he woke on the sofa, lights still blazing from the night before, fully clothed and still drunk.

"Shit!" he stumbled off the sofa and slowly started to pull himself together. Coffee, shower, clothes, he moved as if on autopilot and it wasn't until he entered the bedroom and saw Sophie curled up with her back to him that the horrific reality of the previous night hit him.

"Sweetheart, I'm so, so, sorry if I frightened you last night, I didn't mean to." He slowly approached the bed and sat on his empty side, she didn't move. He noticed she had changed the bed linen, then he realized why she'd had to.

"Soph," he reached for her and she shrugged him off.

"Don't touch me."

"Please hun, I'm really sorry."

"You raped me do you understand? You raped me, sorry doesn't really cut it this time."

"That's a bit harsh, I got carried away and was a bit enthusiastic but I'm not a rapist. Is that what you really think?... Holy shit, you do don't you?"

She spun round and sat up glaring at him.

"What's happened to you? I don't even know you anymore, you raped me you bastard, and you know it."

He stood and in exasperation he wiped his hand over his face, his head was thumping, "I'm going now, we'll talk later. I love you."

"Piss off."

He felt a cold shiver and began to realize how bad things had become between them, how much damage one rash act had caused. Leaving the house and getting into his demo, ironically he was one of the salesmen issued with a 'family car', he acknowledged that he was blatantly over the limit and would have to be especially careful driving to work. Fortunately the dealership was only about fifteen minutes away, although at this time of day that could easily take forty-five minutes. He reached for two pieces of chewing-gum to try and alleviate the vile after-taste left by the night before. It didn't work physically or emotionally.

* * *

It was not even properly light and was grey, drizzly and depressing, typical January. Business was slow, post Christmas lack of funds, people couldn't afford the essentials let alone a new car. It occurred to him with blinding resonance that he was failing to fulfill his commitments at home and at work. He just couldn't perform as expected.

"Shit," he muttered, shaking his head.

"How did I get to this?" In an effort to lift his dreary mood and sober up he cranked up the radio and cracked open the window for the remainder of his crawl through the traffic.

"Hi mate, Christ you look like shit, what's that all about? Don't let his lordship see you or he'll have your balls, he's on one already." Tom's colleague Andy looked up from his desk as Tom walked past. "Fuck off."

"Oy, no need for that. Coffee's on your desk."

Tom continued the walk to his desk at the end of the showroom. Andy was his mate in and out of work and whoever got in first always got the coffees. As he sat down he noticed Andy had followed him and was now perched on his desk.

"Seriously, you ok?"

"No, I'm hung-over. Just some probs at home. Had a big barney last night and slept on the sofa."

"You'll sort it though right? You two will be ok, bunch of flowers, some chocs, works a treat."

He laughed bitterly. "Gonna take more than that to get me out of the dog house this time but hey, I'll sort it. Look out shit-head's coming."

"Tom, a word." The Dealer Principal, known as SJ, a short Scot with a ferocious temper walked past Tom's desk barely pausing to look in Tom's direction. Tom rose and followed him to his small office at the end of the showroom.

By the time Tom had caught up with him he was seated behind his enormous oak desk. Tom stood sheepishly.

"Quite frankly I don't know what the fuck you do with your time. Your figures are shite. Pull your fucking finger out or you'll be out on your fucking ear. Understand?"

"Yes Sir."

"Don't attempt any pathetic excuses, A I don't give a shit and B I'm not fucking listening. Piss off and sell something."

Tom left the office feeling worse than ever. He hadn't been selling anything for far too long. Sophie had been muttering about IVF and the way things were going he wouldn't be able to afford that in the foreseeable future.

Andy was with a middle-aged couple apparently interested in one of the cheaper models. Typical, the first punters of the day and he was with his lordship getting a bollocking. Andy glanced up as he passed giving him a brief quizzical smile. He'd want to hear all the gory details over lunch.

* * *

As soon as she heard the front door close Sophie buried her face in the pillow, she fully expected to cry, she wanted to, she felt like it but she was just too exhausted to manage anything bar a small anguished sob.

She felt hurt, shocked and numb. If someone had told her that Tom would ever have forced himself on her in any way she would have bet her life that it would never happen. Disappointed and disillusioned she made her way to the bathroom and discovered there were bruises on her inner thighs, actual bruises, she had really fought him and yet the man she loved more than anything had physically and sexually assaulted her.

For the briefest of milliseconds she considered phoning the police but it passed just as quickly. If she were to contemplate splitting up then who would father her baby? She'd be single again and that would be a disaster. Resignedly she realized despite last night Tom was a good man and more importantly, her best chance of conception. Second husbands were often vasectomised or didn't want more kids so better to stick with him, and after all she did love him.

With a huge sigh she pondered her plan, she could manipulate him more easily now he was on a major guilt trip, maybe this was for the best, a few bruises were a small price to pay to become a mum.

Feeling her mood lift slightly she began to believe everything that had happened the previous night had happened for a reason and this was just another step towards becoming a family.

* * *

The ringing phone woke her. She was exhausted. She knew she had shocked him but she didn't care, he needed to know how bad things really were and what he'd done to her. The emotional strain was draining her but she kept telling herself she had to focus on her goal. Things would settle down between them once they conceived and if not then so be it, she'd be fine on her own.

"Hello?"

"Sophie, hi, it's Samantha from work, sorry to ring you but I wondered if you were coming back this week? I wouldn't ring but with Kirsty off sick we really need to know where we're at with staffing."

"Kirsty's not ill, she's having an abortion."

"Sophie! That's none of our business is it? She's signed off by a doctor, that's all I need to know. Unfortunately, you're not. What exactly is wrong with you?"

She squirmed with indignation, that cow was murdering a baby in some high priced clinic and *she* was being made to feel guilty. Unbelievable. Tears sprang to her eyes, she fought to hide the emotion in her voice.

"I have sickness and diarrhoea and I won't be back until Monday. Sorry." With that she put the phone down. Within minutes it rang again and, ignoring it, she ran to the bathroom crying.

"Shit, shit, shit," losing her job would mean no chance of IVF; they might even lose the house.

"Calm down, it's ok, calm down." Taking deep breaths she got her breathing and her tears under control.

1471 told her the head of department Samantha had phoned her back; taking a deep breath she pressed three.

"Hi, it's Sophie. I'm so sorry I hung up I had to rush to the loo. Still being sick I'm afraid."

"I did wonder what had happened I must say, I was more than a little surprised at your behavior. Not like you at all, Sophie."

"I know, I've been up all night, I'd just dropped off when you rang, didn't mean to be a bitch, I just feel like crap."

"Don't worry; I'm sorry I woke you. Take care of yourself, see you Monday."

She let out a huge sigh, had she done enough arse-licking to make up for her comments? Probably. She hoped so.

CHAPTER 2

A grim, tedious Wednesday ended with only the nose-to-tail crawl through the rush hour traffic to look forward to. It was sleeting and bitterly cold. He stopped at the traffic-lights by the bus-stop outside the car showroom, its huge glass windows, floor to ceiling mirrors and fantastic state of the art lighting blazing through the winter evening. The cars looked amazing, highly polished, dazzling and unfortunately the last thing anyone wanted to buy, especially from him at the moment. As he stared into the showroom his eyes swept pass the crowd at the bus-stop and he suddenly recognized the girl in the queue. She worked in one of the offices, in the accounts, he only knew her to say hello to but, Jesus it was a vile night and he was going her way. Quickly before the lights changed he opened the passenger window and called out. "Hello, hi, do you want a lift?"

Freezing air flooded in as she bent to look in the window, curious, not recognizing either driver or car. Suddenly she smiled as she realized she did know this man.

"That would be great, thanks."

As she climbed in he attempted to help her with her umbrella and bag acutely aware of the imminent light change, but only succeeded in hitting himself in the face with the wet brolley and touching her thigh.

"Oh shit, sorry, oh bloody hell the lights have changed, hold on, you ok with the seat-belt? I've got to go."

She laughed and it was so relaxed and natural he found himself laughing too.

"No worries, it's really kind of you to pick me up, thanks. Where are you headed?"

"I live in Norden, what about you?"

"Me too, that's spooky! I live just behind the bus station, Summerton Road."

"That's handy; I live just past there in Down-ton Avenue."

"Lucky me, thanks again. I'm Lucy by the way. I've seen you around but don't think we've been introduced."

"I'm Tom, Tom Wilkes. Nice to meet you, you work upstairs right?"

"Yes. I do the purchase ledger, it's ok, pays the bills I guess. My mum used to give me a lift up until last week but she's changed her job so it's the bus for me which is ok in the summer but a bit pants in this crappy weather."

He laughed, suddenly aware of how relaxed he felt in her company, without hesitation he voiced an idea.

"Why don't we car share? I go past your road twice a day and the company pays for the fuel so why not use it to get both of us to work? Give 'em their money's worth as it were?"

"Erm, that would be great. Are you sure?"

"Course, no point in you bussing it when we'll probably be sat in the same traffic jams twice a day."

"Ok then, thanks. What time?"

"I'll pick you up at ten past eight at the end of your road. Ok?"

"Ok."

They sat in a comfortable silence with just the hum of the traffic and the constant swish of the wipers to accompany their slow progress through the London rush hour.

She smelt really amazing, a perfume he hadn't come across before, it was a bit strong but really nice. Up close he became aware of the length of her skirt, or rather the short-ness of it, he remembered how his hand had brushed her thigh and found himself blushing, thank God it was dark. He cursed himself. It was ok to look at pretty girls, to admire them, to fancy them; he was married and had no in-tention of being unfaithful in anything other than fantasy and imagination. This girl was way too young for him, probably only late teens or early twenties, but he liked her straight away and felt relaxed in her company, friends would be a good thing, company for the journey too. No harm no foul.

"Here you go." He pulled over, "see you in the morning."

"Thanks, Tom have a nice evening, see you."

He watched her walk to her door and told him-self he was just seeing her in, just taking care, waiting for a break in the traffic to pull out, but he knew he was enjoying watching her walk away, watching her legs, her arse. He berated himself, "shit man, pack it in. You got some se-rious talking to do at home tonight. Pack it in. Behave yourself." But he was grinning all the way home.

* * *

She heard his key in the lock and a wave of nausea broke over her. She realized she was scared.

"Soph?"

"In here," she called from the kitchen, at least she was home and even better she was talking to him.

He bent to kiss her and she let him find her cheek. He was overwhelmed with relief.

They stood in the kitchen both too nervous to speak, avoiding each other's gaze. The kettle clicked off and Sophie moved to make the coffee.

"I'm really sorry, you know, I just wanted you so much I couldn't wait. It's a compliment I guess," he muttered sheepishly.

He hung his head and ran his hand along the edge of the worktop. He reminded her of a naughty schoolboy and for a moment her heart started to melt and she wanted nothing more than to hold him and be held by him. She started towards him and instantly felt the tender bruising on her thighs and knew that moment of understanding had passed.

"I don't want to talk about it. It was horrid, you hurt me, it's over. I can't forget but I can move on. I have more important things to think about. You let your cock rule your head, typical man, no surprise there but don't ever tell me or yourself what you did was a compliment, that's an insult to me and a cop out for you….coffee?"

"What?… Oh, yes please. I didn't mean it like that I just can't cope with screwing to order, I want to make love to my wife when I, sorry we, feel like it. I'm not a bloody machine. I love you, Sophie."

"And if *I* didn't love *you* I'd have rung the police by now, think of that."

"The police? What the fuck?"

"Look you bastard." She lifted her skirt and exposed her purple, mottled, swollen, bruised thighs.

"Oh shit…oh God…hun, I am so, so, sorry. Shit, Soph I really didn't think I'd hurt you." He collapsed into a kitchen chair, head in hands.

"Well you did, more than you know." She turned away from him and allowed herself a smile.

"I forgive you, ok? Let's move on."

"Thank you, I don't deserve you. I love you so much." He raised his head and she met his gaze.

"Come here," her tone softening. She took him in her arms and let him kiss her neck and forehead.

"I swear I'll never hurt you again sweetheart. I made a terrible mistake, it won't happen again."

"I know."

She smiled, and his relief was almost palpable.

* * *

Snow had fallen over night and by eight the next morning traffic was barely moving. He felt himself becoming agitated in case he let Lucy down. She would think him a total shit if he didn't turn up especially in this weather. He realized they should have exchanged mobile numbers for the rare occasions when either one of them was held up or ill. At eight twelve he saw her at the corner. He honked the horn and she waved.

"Oh my God, it's freezing," she said as she hopped into the car and began to remove her gloves and scarf, and he noted with disappointment she was wearing a longer skirt.

"I know, I'm so sorry I was late. The frigging traffic is awful."

"No worries. You'd think with all the schools closed and a limited bus service it would be easier to get to work."

"Mmm I'll believe it when I see it. I was just thinking we should exchange mobile numbers in case one of us is ever held up. If you don't mind me having your number that is?"

She giggled, "why should I mind, can't I trust you? Are you gonna turn into a stalker or something?"

He grinned, "funny you should say that."

"Oh shit, not another one, just got rid of the last one."

They both burst out laughing and any hint of tension was dissolved.

"Here give me your phone and I'll put my number in whilst you're driving."

"Ok hang on, it's in my trouser pocket." Tom stopped at traffic lights and began to lift up from his seat, struggling to get his phone. "Nearly there, oh shit the lights are changing." He started to pull away.

"Hold on, lift up, I'll get it for you." Lucy leaned over and thrust her hand into his trouser pocket. Tom involuntarily gasped.

"Sorry, didn't mean to make you jump." She moved away instantly blushing.

"It's ok, my fault, I was concentrating on the traffic, sorry," he lied. "It's fine, you carry on, how often does a pretty girl ask to stick her hand in my pocket, best offer I've had all week."

"I find that hard to believe." She grinned and slowly eased her hand into his pocket. In the few moments it took for Lucy to reach the phone Tom was fully hard, embarrassingly so in fact. If she noticed she didn't say and he was grateful. She spent the next few minutes adding their numbers to each other's phones, and his erection began to subside.

As they crawled through the traffic she began to sing along to the radio without a hint of self-consciousness and he found himself joining in. He felt relaxed and it surprised him.

* * *

For the first time in many months he felt happy going into work, he got coffee for himself and Andy and although the weather was atrocious he figured that anyone venturing out to look at cars in the snow must be serious about buying, all he had to do was get to them before anyone else.

By lunchtime he had sold a small hatchback and he was feeling good when Andy stopped by his desk.

"Blimey mate, what's got into you? You're very cheerful today. Sort things out with Sophie then?"

"Sophie?" he realized she hadn't entered his mind all morning.

"Yeh, all sorted thanks. You going out for lunch?"

"Sod off, too bloody cold. I'll get a sarnie out of the machine, you want anything? Nice deal you did this morning saw that bloke come in and before I could blink you were there."

"Just as well after yesterday, bollock-chops had me by the by the short and curlies. Bastard!"

* * *

Just after five thirty Lucy appeared at the end of the showroom looking shy, he stood and beckoned her down. She waved and started towards his desk. "Wasn't sure if I was supposed to meet you here or not."

"Here's fine. Good day?"

"Ok I guess, you?"

"Actually yes, sold one, couple of test drives lined up, not bad for this time of year."

"That's great." She beamed at him and he found himself smiling back. They walked to the car-park chatting comfortably. Once in the car Tom automatically put the radio on and then instantly switched it off. "Sorry that was really rude."

"Don't be daft, course it wasn't, you carry on, the music's fine just one request though."

He pulled into the traffic, "go on."

"Not radio two please; it may age me before my time."

He burst out laughing, gesturing towards the radio.

"Cheeky cow. Help yourself."

Grinning, she quickly located Capital Radio and started to hum along. As they made slow progress through the evening rush hour Tom had plenty of opportunity to admire her legs and enjoy her perfume. She sang intermittently, made comic observations and chatted to the radio. Tom listened, smiling, happy to enjoy her company and amused at how easy it was to be with her.

At he pulled over to let her out she leant over and placed her hand on his thigh and pecked him on the cheek.

"Thanks," and before he could respond she was out and walking towards her house. Again, he watched her go but as she reached her front door she turned and waved. Quickly he turned away feeling embarrassed.

"Shit," he muttered, blushing. He was hard again.

Over the following weeks they fell into an easy routine, she chatted, sang to the radio and continued to kiss him on the cheek until it felt normal, friendly and innocent. He, for his part, listened, laughed and generally enjoyed her light-hearted company but still found himself hornier than ever, if she noticed she ignored it, as he tried to. Things at home were strained and tense but Tom found that being with Lucy for a short time each day made him calmer and more confident.

* * *

More snow had fallen and Tom and Andy decided that it was too cold to go to the pub for lunch, so they wandered to the staff room. Choosing their lunches from the vending machine they went to make coffee when Lucy walked in with another of the office staff. She instantly made her way over to him ignoring everyone else. She was grinning, blatantly pleased to see him.

"Hi, Tom how's your day going?"

"Yeh, good thanks, how's yours?"

"Same shit different day really."

They laughed together totally oblivious to the stares of both Andy and Lucy's companion.

"It's unusual to see you here, it's a really nice surprise, you've cheered me up."

"Too cold to go to the pub today, must be a shite day if seeing me can cheer you up. All I can say is you're easily pleased."

"Cheeky git," she playfully punched him in the arm.

"That's it, I'm off, I can't work now, my arm, its agony."

"Ooh you big baby, want me to kiss it better?"

"Ow I think I've hurt me cock can you kiss that better, Luce?" Called one of the mechanics from the other side of the room.

Instantly Tom spun round. "Shut your fucking mouth, Lee."

"Or what?" The mechanic stood up.

"Or I'll shut it for you. Wanker."

"Yeh right!!" Lee sat back down laughing. "Bit sensitive aren't you, Thomas time of the month is it love?"

Lucy grabbed Tom's arm and dragged him from the room leaving Andy speechless. "What a prick. I hate him, I'm sorry he wound you up."

"I was just pissed off he spoke to you like that but you're right he is a prick." They both smiled and the tension ebbed away.

"Come up here a minute." She took his hand and led him through a rabbit warren of small corridors to a boiler-room at the end by the fire-escape.

"I wanted a moment alone to say thanks for picking me up, you know the car sharing and everything, it's gonna save me a bomb in bus fares. Maybe I can take you out for a drink or something sometime to say thanks?"

"That would be great," he said tentatively. "But I am married you know."

"Yes, I know but it's just a drink and I fig-ured that anyone who gets a hard-on from me putting my hand in his pocket can't be all that happy at home," she smiled sheepishly. "I know you watch me walk up to my front door every day."

"I'm just waiting to pull out that's all."

"Mmm ok, whatever you say." Tom blushed.

"I'm a little out of my depth here, I *am* married."

"I know, don't be freaked, I fancy you, you fancy me but we're just friends, it's ok, I just thought you seemed a little..."

"A little what?"

"Well jealous about what Lee said that's all."

"Jealous? Not at all he was just being a low life and you don't deserve to be spoken to like that."

"For what it's worth I was really flattered."

She leant up to peck him on the lips. As they parted they stopped to stare at each other, only inches apart. Then they both leaned in and their lips met again. The kiss lasted, and in the middle of a dusty boiler-room full of spider webs and noise their lips parted and their tongues met.

CHAPTER 3

The clinic was beautiful, stylish, ultra-modern and spotlessly clean. Kirsty sat in the waiting area looking terrified.

"You'll be fine love; you're doing the right thing."

The young man next to her put a comforting arm round her shoulders, although he was clearly as distressed as she was.

"Then why do I feel so shit?"

"That's obvious, but you don't have a choice."

"Maybe we could just have it?"

"This little one would never survive, we know this, she's got too much wrong with her."

"I know but I love her."

"Me too."

She folded into his arms and started to cry.

"Kirsty Millson please." A smartly dressed nurse appeared from the treatment room.

Kirsty raised her tear-stained face, she was white with fear. They both stood and Alex and Kirsty walked hand in hand towards the treatment room to say goodbye to a much wanted and already loved pregnancy.

Kirsty's twelve week scan had showed huge birth defects and a child that, if born, would probably not survive so her GP had referred her to a private clinic to try and reduce the trauma. She'd confided in her office manager; Sophie, and her department head; Samantha, she'd pretended to be so blasé so matter of fact. Inside her heart was breaking. Alex had been so good but they were both devastated. Even as she signed the consent form tears dripped on the page. She knew, they both did, that she might never get over this day.

* * *

Tom grabbed Lucy's buttocks and pulled her into his body. She felt his erection and pushed against it. His hand went to her breast and she gasped. "Fuck me."

His other hand found her thong, she was soaking wet and as he slid his fingers into her she bore down on them. His thumb found her clitoris and within seconds she was in the throes of orgasm.

"I want you, please," she moaned as she thrust against his hand. Silently but breathlessly he spun them both round so her back was to the wall, without breaking eye contact she undid his trousers and reached for his penis. Freeing him she started to rub him.

"Stop. Oh shit. No. Stop," he moved her hand. "I want to come inside you not in your hand."

She grinned, "God, I want you."

"Turn round," he whispered breathlessly.

As she turned and leant over he guided himself into her hot depths and instantly they both came, she was so wet and warm he was totally lost in the moment, her beautiful arse, one hand on her soft breast, the other between her legs rubbing her.

Amazingly, he stayed hard and they began to move together. "You are gorgeous, so fucking wet and tight. I'm still hard."

"Mmm, don't stop."

He rubbed her clitoris until he felt her clench and shudder and as she came again and again he let go a second time. They had no concept of time, both completely lost in the sensuousness of the experience.

He wanted to turn her round to look at her face and kiss her but he really didn't want to pull out of her. Eventually, as their panting subsided he began to soften.

"It's going to sleep," she giggled and he slipped out.

"Bugger, I could have stayed in there all afternoon."

"I wish."

She turned and they kissed.

"Surprised you didn't freeze your pussy in that little thong in this weather."

"Thinking about you keeps my pussy warm, don't worry about that."

"You're a saucy minx."

"You bet."

"Oh my God, you're so sexy, I've only known you a few weeks and after that I feel like I can't keep my hands off you. Shit, I just cheated and I never felt so good." He was grinning from ear to ear.

"Please don't think I planned this, but after noticing you fancied me as much as I fancy you it just seemed the right thing to do. Standing up to Lee like that made me so horny I just wanted you," she stroked his face.

"Shame we're at work, think I could go again, you're so fucking hot. Better get dressed though." He checked his watch.

"Bollocks, it's two already. You go out first, I'll nip down the fire-escape and go round the back through parts and service. Give us a kiss."

The kiss lasted longer than anticipated and when his thumb found her nipple she jumped back. "Oy you, no, we'll be missed."

"Well, I'll miss *you*, that's for sure."

Grinning cheekily she slipped out of the boiler room and down the corridor towards the Ladies.

* * *

Desperately trying to look calm and professional he adjusted his clothes and combed his hair with his fingers until he realized that he hadn't washed his hands. Smiling he sniffed his fingers and felt himself getting hard, he licked his fingers and thought of licking her.

"Gents first I think," he muttered as he headed for the toilets.

* * *

Checking his mobile he noticed he had several missed calls and a text from Andy.

'Where r u? R u doing wot I think u r doing u jammy bastard lol.'

He grinned, didn't take long for his mate to suss him out. He supposed the rest of the building would know by five thirty too. Tough. They would just deny everything. Gossip counted for nothing. Suddenly a thought stopped him in his tracks. What if Lucy told anyone? Reaching for his mobile he text her, 'don't tell anyone about lunch-time our secret c u at 5.30 my desk' now the real dilemma, kisses or no kisses? He decided against it.

"You bastard."

Andy was grinning from ear to ear.

"No idea what you mean."

"Yeh right, looking at your grin I reckon you got a quick fumble for your trouble."

"Shut up shit-head, keep your voice down."

Tom leant over Andy's desk, "would be better if everyone this side of Clapham common didn't find out thanks," he whispered.

"Sorry mate. You are so jammy though, luscious lunchtime fuck-buddy at work and the gorgeous Sophie waiting for you, keeping it hot, and wet for that matter, at home. Poor Sophie have you no scruples?"

"Not exactly like that at home, not everything's rosy mate, trust me what you see isn't always what you get."

"Anything to do with that big row you had? Don't tell me you shagged that lass just to get back at Sophie? For Christ's sake she's your wife."

"Of course not, it's complicated ok? Things are shit at home and Lucy just happened to be there, on a plate as it were, she's absolutely gorgeous I tell you, totally willing and gorgeous. You would've."

"Chance would be a fine thing. The difference is, I'm single."

"What's really weird is I don't feel that guilty. I thought if I ever thought about screwing around the guilt would put me off straight away."

"Maybe that's just because things aren't great at home?"

"Maybe, right here, right now if I had to choose between the control freak, hormonally charged, baby obsessed, sperm grabbing wife and the juicy Lucy fuck-buddy I would leave Soph in a heartbeat."

"That's just because you're still horny and wet from the aforementioned Lucy's juice."

They both burst out laughing, "damn right I am."

* * *

At five thirty-two he looked up from his desk, Lucy was walking towards him. She was stunning. She grinned at him and mouthed "hi sexy" despite himself he grinned back. She reached his desk and perched on the edge. "Ready?" Standing he grabbed his coat and they headed for the car-park.

Once in the car she reached over to kiss him and he slid his hand up her skirt.

"Oh God, you're so gorgeous."

He nuzzled her neck and slipped a finger into her.

"Oh that's good, but shouldn't we go somewhere a bit more private? Someone will see."

"Good point."

Reluctantly withdrawing, he kissed her and then started the car.

He could feel her moisture on his finger and became aware of the smell of sex from his hand. His erection was almost unbearable. Taking her hand he placed it over his flies. "See what you're doing to me."

She giggled, "where are we going? Not far I hope."

"No not far."

Ten minutes later he pulled into a dark back alley between two factories.

"Bring all your girlfriends here do you?" She joked but he was totally focused on her.

"Put the seat back...that's it."

He leaned over her and lifted her skirt. Hooking her thong to the side he bent to run his tongue over her. She moaned and opened her legs as wide as possible. He reached up and flicked on the interior light. He gazed down and bent to kiss her. "Beautiful, pink, and wet, mmm you're so fucking gorgeous." He began lapping at her and as he slid two fingers into the warm wet depths of her she came again and again.

Finally calmer she reached for him.

"Your turn I think," and as she released him she bent to take him in her mouth.

"Oh shit that's good, hang on….just a minute." She stopped to look at him. His eyes were closed and he was biting his lower lip.

"I'm gonna come in a minute."

"That's ok."

"No, it's feels gorgeous but I wanna come inside you. Get on top."

She maneuvered herself past the gearstick and handbrake and straddled him. The instant he felt her envelope him he let out a huge groan and started to orgasm. She put her hand down and began to rub her clitoris until she orgasmed with him.

* * *

Tom and Sophie by some unspoken but seemingly mutual agreement settled into silence about the rape. The bruises faded and, it seemed, so did her anger. He knew she was checking the dates and once the ovulation predictor gave the go-ahead he would be in demand again. They went to work, made polite conversation, they kissed each other on the cheek, but the stress remained. He sensed that despite the relative calm she was still utterly focused on her plans.

* * *

Quickly she undid the packaging. Ten pairs of loose cotton boxer shorts. Perfect. She removed all his briefs and close fitting shorts from the drawer and put them in a black bin-bag. She replaced them with the new ones and closed the drawer, finally satisfied. She knew once the black bag was in the outside bin he'd have no choice but to wear the ones she'd had delivered. She smiled.

* * *

Having dropped Lucy off he drove to the nearest filling-station. Making his way to the toilet, he knew he'd have to wash and freshen up before heading home. He washed his hands, face, penis and balls. He decided to pick up some baby-wipes to keep in the car. Standing in the queue to pay he glanced at the condoms. His blood ran cold, he'd never even thought about contraception or safe sex. Stupid bastard he thought. It had been so long since he'd had to worry about that. Shit what if Lucy wasn't on the pill, what about STI's. He'd watched enough episodes of embarrassing teenage bodies to know the risks were high amongst teenagers. He'd never thought that watching that programme to see naked girls had actually taught him anything. Teenager? He thought, how old was she? Oh shit, one can of worms after another. He paid for the petrol and baby-wipes and was walking back to the car when his phone went off twice. Looking down he had two texts.

'Where r u?' From Sophie and an MMS from Lucy. He opened the message and was greeted by a picture of her wearing black lace underwear including stockings and suspenders.

'U like?' It read. Oh shit, no contest. He text Lucy back, 'OMFG yeh!!' With two kisses and Sophie back with 'home in 10' with none.

* * *

"Sorry I'm late," he called from the front door. He noted that dinner seemed to be cooking and it smelt really good. He shot up the stairs before she could answer and immediately took a shower. Thinking about his day made him hard all over again. He closed his eyes and thought of Lucy's tight little pussy.

"Tom, what are you doing in the shower? Dinner's ready."

"Just a minute."

Sophie entered the bathroom and even through the steam and the condensation on the shower screen she could see his erection. Backing away she quickly left the room. She covered her face with her hands. If she was that scared of him how would they ever get pregnant? The bruising was fading but she still felt deeply shocked by the rape. She knew she could never fully trust Tom again. Things had changed forever.

He walked out onto the landing wrapped in a towel, "you ok?" He asked casually. He took in her anxious look and the way she held her hands over her mouth and went to take her in his arms. Hastily she moved away, "fine thanks, just tired."

Instantly he realized she was scared and he took her in his arms and looked into her eyes. "Soph, what happened that night, don't let it come between us."

"Too late I'm afraid."

"Oh come on, I said I was sorry and I meant it."

Refusing to meet his gaze she stared at the floor. "Let me go please or are you planning a repeat performance?"

He let her go and turned towards the bedroom. "Hardly, you're probably not bloody ovulating yet."

"You bastard."

"Piss off, Soph you're so fucking perfect, you never made a mistake I'll bet."

"It's my fault now then?"

Opening his drawer he pulled out the new boxers.

"Er, excuse me but where are my pants and what are these?"

He threw the boxers onto the landing floor.

"I thought you could do with some new ones that's all."

"Where are my pants? I bloody hate these and why are you buying me underwear, you're not my mother."

"Your pants are in the bin."

"What have you done?"

"You need to change to these to keep your testicles cool, to help us conceive, we talked about it."

"You asked me and I said no, I don't like my balls swinging in the breeze thank you."

"It's only some pants for God's sake and, let's face it, you owe me."

"Oh, so that's it is it? You chuck some of clothes and take away my choice and I'm supposed to suck it up because you say I raped you."

"YOU DID!" She screamed. "YOU FUCKING DID and it really hurt and I was really scared." Sliding down the wall she started to sob. He rubbed his face with his hands, what a mess.

"I really am sorry, but you can't just bin my stuff. Soph, don't cry, please."

"It's just some underpants get over it," her tears quickly turning to anger.

"Actually it's not just some underpants it's my whole sodding life, wear this, don't wank, have sex now, don't have sex now, don't touch me yet, touch me right now. I am so fucking sick of this."

"And I love it I guess?"

"No, but you want it...I don't."

"AND THERE WE HAVE IT," she shouted. "THE TRUTH."

"I will not play your game, Sophie I will not live like this." He walked into the bedroom and slammed the door shut. He was breathing heavily and shaking.

"Calm down, calm down," he whispered to himself. He picked up his phone and text Andy.

* * *

Sophie stumbled downstairs to the kitchen. Picking up the saucepan of chili she threw it across the room where it hit the wall.

"YOU BASTARD. I HATE YOU," she screamed as she buried her face in her hands and started to cry. "Oh, Tom." Reaching for the vodka she took a gulp.

CHAPTER 4

"There will be more bleeding and it may be heavy at times, that's to be expected, you should continue to lose the pregnancy over the next few hours. Take paracetamol and contact your nearest A&E if the pain suddenly gets worse or you start to feel feverish or run a temperature."

The nurse was very kind and reassuring but Kirsty felt cold and detached from the whole situation.

She'd been given the oral medication two days before, followed by hormone pessaries early that morning and had started to have pain and bleeding some time after. They'd made her use a bedpan throughout the day and they'd examined the contents for evidence that she'd passed the pregnancy.

She'd kept her eyes shut every time she'd used the bedpan, she didn't want to see what she'd passed. Her imagination was doing that for her.

Alex had stayed with her all day in the en-suite room, holding her hand, talking to her, holding her when she'd cried. It had helped, but not much. Walking to the car with a huge sanitary towel between her legs she felt so lost and alone. She couldn't escape the feeling she'd killed her child.

Alex put her in the car and put the seat-belt round her.

"We did the right thing sweetheart."

She didn't reply just stared out into the snowy afternoon. All the drive home he held her hand and when they arrived at their flat he undid her seat-belt and led her through the front door and sat her in the lounge. His phone bleeped. Pulling it from his pocket he read the text. "It's Luce she sends you lotsa love and hugs and says ring her anytime day or night and she'll pop and see you tomorrow. I'll text her thanks yeh?"

"Yeh, that's fine."

'Hi Kirsty's nt gud mate. Ruff day. Feeling shit myself. Cu 2moz x' he hit send.

"It won't help but let's put the fire on, make a cuppa and snuggle up?"

She looked up into his tear filled blue eyes and knew why she loved him.

"Yes please."

* * *

His phone bleeped, it was Tom, 'fancy a pint. Cud do with a chat' he checked his watch and text back 'kwl cu at the dog in 45.'

Andy showered and changed and, grabbing his keys and wallet left his flat thirty minutes later. Their pub of choice 'The Dog' was roughly fifteen minutes from both their homes and therefore they could both drink and walk home. Andy assumed he was about to hear all about Tom's lunchtime fumble in all its glory.

Tom had arrived first and was ordering two pints when Andy walked in.

"Alright? Cheers." Both took a huge swig and made their way towards their usual table.

"C'mon then, I wanna hear it all, every gory detail."

"Ha, you must be joking...although, trust me, she's amazing, totally amazing and she came onto me really." Andy's eyebrows shot up.

"I mean it; she was so up for it was a done deal by the time we got to the boiler-room."

"Ah I wondered where you were. I'd have bet on the disabled loo."

Tom laughed, "I'll keep that in mind, that's not why I wanted a chat though."

"Ok, shall I guess, it's about you and Sophie right?"

"Why do you say that?"

"Well you had a massive barney the other night and you're now cheating with a lass from work. It doesn't look good does it?"

"It's such a fucking mess. Things have been bad for about a year. Soph wants a baby, I mean really badly, to the point where everything we do is about getting pregnant. We don't eat certain things in case it reduces our fertility, we can't shag unless she's ovulating, no unnecessary sex, only certain positions and when she comes on, well it's like the end of the bloody world, and you know what? I get it, I really do, she wants kids but I am so sick of living with this constant pressure to perform to order. I want a normal life and I want my wife back. We don't make love, we don't shag we don't even snog unless she's ovulating. I feel like a sperm donor and I hate it."

"Shit mate, I had no idea things were that bad. Have you had any tests?"

"That's the point we tried for six months and she marched us off to the GP who told us to relax and try for another year."

"And how long ago was that?"

"Eight months."

"Shit, not looking good then?"

"No, but that's not why we argued. I try to be really supportive, I say all the right things every month, I perform when instructed, I dry her tears, I make all the right noises but a couple of weeks ago I really lost it I didn't just overstep the mark I ran straight across it at high speed."

"Go on."

"I raped her."

Andy spluttered. "What?"

"I know it sounds awful but I just wanted to be in charge for once, I wanted to fuck my wife, I was horny and I just got sick of the whole abstinence thing and I forced her."

"Shit, what were you thinking?"

"Well, actually I wasn't thinking, my dick was doing all the thinking and he said let's do it, so I did it. Turns out I hurt her, bruised her really more than anything, and what's really shit is she's scared of me, she's really scared I can see it in her face."

"I'm not fucking surprised, you bastard, I love you like a brother but this...you were well out of order."

Andy pushed his seat back from the table as if to distance himself from Tom's confession.

"I know, don't you think I feel like a total arsehole? Tonight I found out she'd replaced my pants with loose boxers cause they help with male fertility and I completely overreacted, threw a right paddy."

"So to make up for being a complete wanker you decided to shag some little tart at work? Who are you? Again, what were you thinking?"

"And again, I wasn't, it was all dick driven. It's such a mess."

"I'm going outside for a fag, I'll have a double JD and it's your round. I need to think."

After ten minutes and several cigarettes later Andy re-entered the bar and sat down.

"Sorry mate, I was a bit quick to have a go at you, I don't know how I'd react if I'd been going through this for over a year. You were out of order but I think I understand."

Tom let out a huge sigh; he hung his head in his hands. "That means a lot, thanks, believe me you can't hate me more than I do."

"So, this lass at work, what's happening there?"

"God knows, she's gorgeous and she wants me, I shagged her 'cause I could I guess, bit shit on her though."

"Far be it from me to be the killjoy again but please tell me you used a condom."

Andy took one look at Tom's face and threw up his hands in disgust. "You dick, so let's hope she's on the pill and clean then otherwise you'll be giving Sophie a very unexpected pressie. Ok please tell me you only shagged her once."

"Mmm I can't."

"Shit mate, if you had a brain cell it would die of fucking loneliness. You knob."

"I get it ok, in the past week I have completely screwed up my marriage, potentially screwed up my job, and turned into a STI carrying rapist. Fucking ace."

"Very funny but as I see it there's only one issue here and that's are you gonna try and patch things up with Soph or are you gonna walk away from ten years of marriage? Do you still love her? Do you want kids?"

"If kids come along then great, if not that's ok too. Yes I love her but I'm not *in* love with her. If you'd asked me two years ago I would have said with absolute certainty that I was totally in love with her but now...I don't even know if she loves me."

"Well, if she doesn't she's taking a lot of shit off you mate. That must tell you something. How do you feel about your little fuck-buddy?"

"Feel? Horny, dirty, lucky, grateful. Seriously, she's great, the sex blows my mind, and, although I hardly know her I feel so relaxed with her. Totally chilled, she's fun and funny. If I'd met her in another life, she'd probably be the one."

"Shit, that's not what I wanted or expected to hear. Really? You've only known her a few weeks."

"I know, I don't remember feeling like that with Soph, ever, that's scary."

"You *are* in the shit mate."

"I know, maybe I should leave Soph and just be on my own for a bit, but I can't help thinking that as soon as we get pregnant things will be great again, like they were, the really scary thing is how bad will things be if we don't get pregnant, ever?"

* * *

Lucy took off the lace underwear and slipped into joggers and a hoodie. She could still remember Tom's kiss, his fingers, his tongue, his cock, she began to tingle. Everything in her head was screaming a warning, 'he's married, it won't come to anything, walk away' but she knew she couldn't. She cared about him, couldn't stop thinking about him and it really scared her.

CHAPTER 5

He opened the front door and took a deep breath. The house was quiet although the downstairs lights were on. Silently he walked from room to room but the ground floor was empty. As he entered the kitchen he saw the pan on the floor and the huge red stain cascading down the wall.

"Bollocks," he muttered. For a second he deliberated about clearing the mess up before venturing upstairs but thought he'd better speak to Sophie first.

Taking each stair as quietly as possible he reached the landing, and again every light was blazing. Stopping to listen he became aware that the shower was running. He opened the bathroom door and saw her sitting in the shower fully clothed. She'd obviously been crying but was now gazing into the middle distance.

He was completely shocked.

With his voice breaking with emotion he whispered, "Soph...honey, come here."

She looked up, suddenly aware of his presence. He reached in to turn the water off to find it had run cold.

"Oh my God, you're freezing. Let's get you dry."

Wrapping her in a bath sheet he helped her stand and step out. She was bitterly cold and soaked through, probably drunk, he guessed. He stripped her wet clothes from her and started rubbing her arms and back to warm her. Slowly she turned her head to look at him. "Why are you doing this?"

"Because you're my wife and I love you. Listen sweetheart I'm so sorry for how I've behaved, let's try and make this work huh?"

She started to cry silently. He led her to their bed, laid her down and covered her with the quilt before getting in next to her.

"Look at me." He reached over and drew her chin towards him. "Look at me, Soph we're gonna make this work, we're gonna have kids and grow old together, trust me."

"I want to, Tom but I don't know how to get back to where we were."

"Let me show you."

He started by caressing her back and slowly as she relaxed he moved down to her buttocks. "I'll never hurt you again, I swear, please trust me."

His mouth found her nipple and instantly she stiffened, "relax hun, it's ok, we'll go at your pace and I'll stop whenever you want me to ok?"

"I don't know."

"Trust me." He leant down and kissed her gently, tenderly and with such love she started to soften and respond.

He was already hard but he knew he had to take his time, rolling her onto her back he traced his tongue down her stomach and as he parted her thighs he softly kissed each fading bruise and with each kiss he whispered, "forgive me, forgive me, forgive me."

As his tongue found her clitoris she arched off the mattress. Slowly he slid a finger into her, despite her anxiety she was beautifully wet, he lapped at her and felt her body start to shudder.

She took a while to finally give herself over to the orgasm, he worked her with his tongue and finger until eventually her body took over and she was writhing beneath him. Normally as soon as she'd come he would maneuver himself so that he could enter her whilst still rubbing

her as she was coming and they'd come together, but this time was too important so he
waited for her climax to subside and looking her
straight in the eye he slowly entered her. They
both gasped and as he pushed harder she drove
her hips up to meet him all fear gone.

As he thrust into the hot warm depths of her
a picture flashed into his mind and he was suddenly in the car with Lucy, shaking his head he
pulled himself back into the moment. That flash-
back of Lucy was enough to tip him into orgasm
and as he closed his eyes he saw her body, her
face, her pussy.

* * *

She stepped into the car and leant over to kiss
him but he turned his head so she only managed to graze his cheek.

"Is everything ok? Are you alright?"

"Yeh fine." He reached over to crank up the
radio.

She tried to distract him from the traffic, to
make eye contact but he stubbornly refused.

"Tom, look at me, what's up? Have I upset
you? Have I done something wrong?"

The snow from several days before had turned
to slush and the London traffic was still painfully
slow.

At the next red light she turned the radio off
and took his face and turned it towards her.
"Talk to me, please," her eyes were wide with
concern.

"What happened yesterday I'm sorry it was a
mistake, I'm married and ok, things aren't great
but I owe it to Sophie to try again. You're gorgeous and the sex was amazing and I've got a

hard-on just being in the car with you but we can't sleep together again."

For a second she was silent, too shocked to speak, she'd read him so completely wrong.

"Ok, yes that's fine."

The lights changed and he pulled away. "Maybe I'd better get the bus. Pull over."

"Don't be stupid, we're still friends, you're not getting the bus ok?"

"Is that wise? Maybe you shouldn't be alone with me?" The bitterness of her tone stung him.

"Please don't be like that. I'm truly, truly, sorry, I didn't mean to lead you on but let's be honest, you came onto me." The traffic ground to a halt and as it did the car door opened and she disappeared into the crowd.

He quickly pulled over and jumped out. "LUCY, LUCY, shit!"

He rang her mobile, but as expected it went straight to voicemail.

"Bollocks!!" He hit the steering-wheel with the flat of his hand.

"Shit!"

* * *

She ran crying through the crowd into the tube station confident that he wouldn't follow. She stopped by the ticket machine and tried to calm down. The crowd was jostling her as she moved out of the way and into the shadows.

Her phone rang, it was his number. She let it ring.

PART 2
SPRING

CHAPTER 6

Sales were up, the nights were lighter, it was still cold but the snow had passed and weak spring sunshine had taken its place.

Tom hadn't seen Lucy since that morning. She'd left her job at the dealership that day and never returned. The company accountant had asked him if he knew why she'd left so unexpectedly. He said that he had no idea and that he barely knew her anyway. The guilt stung. He'd text her every day for the first week but after that he realized she wasn't going to respond. Life carried on and for a while things ran on an even keel. He and Sophie were having a lot more sex and she seemed calmer, more reassured.

* * *

She came awake vaguely aware of the stickiness between her legs. Throwing back the quilt she peered at the sheet and as she saw the blood she screamed.

"NO! No, no, no." Tom, shocked awake by her scream bolted upright. "What the hell's happened?" But by now she was in the bathroom. He looked at the blood. "Shit." He was at the bathroom door in an instant. "Sweetheart, open the door." She was crying. "Please."

"Leave me alone."

"Open the door, Soph."

"NO!"

Silently he stripped the bed, loaded the washer and put on clean linen. He heard the shower.

He felt none of her disappointment only concern for her. Despite his attempts to empathize his only thought was how this bombshell would affect their relationship.

He was halfway through his second coffee when she got downstairs. Rising he took her in his arms kissing her forehead tenderly.

"It's ok, Tom you don't have to worry. I don't blame you."

He dropped his arms and stepped away, "what for?"

"For stopping trying, for having sex without checking on my cycle, for having me go on top, for spoiling things. Don't worry," she spat bitterly, "its fine, really."

"Hang on, trying for a baby in my book means having lots of sex and also having some kind of normal life and that's what we've had."

"I don't want a normal life I want a baby, I gave you what you wanted and again we're not pregnant."

"It's no-one's fault, it's just the way it is, although of course necking half a bottle of vodka once a month can't help."

Her hand hit him hard on the cheek leaving a red hand print. "You bastard."

"You bitch."

"I hate you." She started to cry.

"No you don't." His voice softened as he took her in his arms.

* * *

Lucy woke with the overpowering urge to vomit. Rushing to the bathroom she just managed to reach the toilet in time. She rinsed her mouth and as she wiped her face she noticed how painful her breasts were.

Feeling slightly better she sat on the edge of the bed and peered at her calendar. Unhooking it from the wall she started to flick between January and February, counting the weeks.

Shaking her head she counted again and again.

"No, no, no, that's not possible."

She checked her pack of pills and realized she was due to start the next packet tomorrow so her period should have arrived. Tipping the rest of the foil packets out of the box she remembered why her calculations might be wrong. She'd gone away for a hen weekend the previous month and had forgotten to take her pills with her so consequently had missed three days out of the pack. Lucy didn't realize whether that meant she was three days out with her maths or three days late with her period. Slipping the information leaflet from the box she started to read and as she read her face paled.

"Oh shit...oh bollocks."

* * *

Tom struggled up the stairs with the breakfast tray, he nudged open the bedroom door and placed it on the bed.

"Morning...wake up sleepyhead." Opening the curtains he frowned as Sophie ducked under the quilt.

"I'm not hungry."

"So. We're having breakfast in bed, make the most of it 'cause when we do have kids this will be a thing of the past."

Her head appeared over the quilt, "don't you mean if?"

"No, when. We have to be positive, I read that visualization is really important in conception, and even if we end up adopting you can still wave goodbye to Sunday mornings like this."

Slowly she smiled. "I love you, Tom Wilkes."

"That's good then 'cause I love you too, Sophie Wilkes." Tom placed the tray on the floor and let his robe fall. He was fully aroused.

"How about a shower before breakfast, Mrs W?"

Taking her hand he led her to the shower. As the water fell he kissed her face, her breasts and her stomach before parting her thighs with his fingers and gently, tenderly stroking her. As he eased his fingers inside her she let out a soft moan. She pushed against his hand and he felt her start to come. "Turn around," he whispered.

She turned to face the wall and as he stroked her clitoris he entered her. They moved together the warm water caressing their bodies, one hand between her legs the other on her breast, thumbing and gently pinching her hard nipple. Suddenly he was back in the boiler-room with Lucy. It was Lucy's body he was looking at, her arse, her nipple he was feeling, her clitoris he was stroking and as he remembered he came.

CHAPTER 7

Kirsty sat down opposite her GP Dr Hayes. She was pale and drawn.

He smiled gently, "how are you doing?"

Silently she started to cry, passing her a tissue he waited until she lifted her head to look at him.

"I feel so lost, so guilty, so hurt."

"That's natural, Kirsty you've been through a terrible ordeal. How's Alex doing?"

"Better than me, he wants to try again."

"That's normal. What do you want?"

"I don't think I ever want to be pregnant again."

"Oh surely you don't mean that, it's early days, far too soon to decide either way."

"I mean it, I can't bear the thought of it happening again, and before you quote me the statistics, I know the chances are so small it's not worth worrying about. The truth is I don't think I'll ever be able to love another baby without feeling guilty about this one, that's no way to start a family."

"That's very honest of you, have you told Alex how you feel?"

"No. He thinks another baby will make us feel better."

"And you think it won't?"

"I know it won't, I want to go back on the pill."

"Ok, well that's no problem but I urge you to talk to Alex." He reached for his prescription pad.

"Better do your blood pressure and weight then."

"I don't know if I can talk to him, he wants to 'get back to normal'," she formed parenthesis in the air with her fingers to emphasize the words.

"And you can't ever imagine that I guess?"

"Exactly."

"Would you consider counselling?"

Stepping off of the scales she sat back down.

"They offered me counselling at the clinic but I said no." Slipping the blood pressure cuff onto her arm he met her gaze.

"Can I ask why?"

"I don't want to talk about it to anyone, not Alex, not you, not my mum, not Lucy and not a counsellor. I killed my baby, the guilt is my punishment, it's what I deserve."

"Oh dear Lord, you're so wrong," he placed his hand over hers.

"Your pregnancy was not viable, how it had lasted to thirteen weeks I don't know, it would not have survived that's a definite, you made the decision to undergo an early termination rather than a late one or worse a full blown labor and delivery of a stillborn baby or a severely disabled child that would have died within a few hours. You did the brave thing, the right thing."

"Then why do I feel like shit?"

"You're grieving, you have had a bereavement, it's natural. You never got to hold your child, you have no photos, no memories and yet it was real and obviously wanted and loved."

She nodded and sobbed, unable to respond as more tears came.

"Might I suggest another two weeks off and maybe some anti-depressants?"

"I don't want anti-depressants but I don't think I can face work yet."

"Ok, but I want to see you in two weeks."

As they stood he hugged her warmly.

"Kirsty, you will get through this I promise, just don't be frightened to take some help."

He had helped her stop smoking, confirmed her pregnancy, seen her through the horrendous scan results, arranged the termination at a private clinic with PCT funding but still felt helpless to ease her pain. She looked so young, so frail.

Leaving the surgery with her prescription she made her way to the chemist opposite.

* * *

The choice was huge, so many kits, all so expensive. She knew in her heart that she was pregnant but she clung to the faint hope that a test might prove her wrong. The vomiting, tender breasts and running to the loo all the time only really meant one thing. With a shaking hand she picked the cheapest, it didn't say how many weeks pregnant you were it just said pregnant or not pregnant, yes or no, smiles or tears.

As she joined the queue she heard her name, "Luce?"

She turned. It was Kirsty. She looked tired and drawn. She had a prescription in her hand but her eyes were on the pregnancy test. "Is that for you?" She asked calmly.

For a second Lucy considered lying but one look at her sister's face and she knew she had to be honest.

"I'm sorry, Kirst; I didn't want you to find out like this."

"It is yours then?"

"Yes."

The queue moved and Lucy reached the checkout, she quickly paid and moved aside to wait for her sister.

"Does mum know?"

"Course not. She'd go mad."

"No shit."

"It wasn't intentional."

"Oh that makes it ok then, it was an accident. You accidentally fell on some bloke's cock without using contraception."

"I went away and forgot to take my pills with me. I didn't realize 'til I was late that I wasn't safe."

Lucy started to cry, "I'm scared, Kirst so scared."

Softening her sister put a comforting arm round her shoulders.

"Come back to mine and do the test there."

"Thanks. I can't imagine how hard this must be for you."

"Shush, let's just get home and have a cup of tea 'cause as mum says, 'a nice cuppa tea makes everything better'."

"That's bollocks." Lucy laughed.

"I know." Her sister smiled back at her and linking arms they made their way back to Kirsty and Alex's.

CHAPTER 8

The digital predictor was smiling at her, which meant one thing. She was ovulating and they had to have sex tonight and preferably tomorrow too.

Tonight she would cook his favorite meal, wear something sexy and together they'd make a baby. She heard Tom getting out of bed and she quickly cleared away the kit. As he entered the bathroom she wondered whether she might be able to persuade him to 'do it' before work, they couldn't do it in the shower because the seminal fluid would run out too easily but she might catch him in the bedroom between his shower and getting dressed. She felt no sexual attraction for her husband, she wasn't turned-on she just wanted to become pregnant.

As Tom entered the bedroom still toweling his hair he felt Sophie behind him and as her arms came round his waist she reached for his cock. She pressed her body into his and purred, "good morning."

"Hi, erm...have you seen my green tie?"

"Not unless you want to tie me up with it, no."

Turning round he took her by the shoulders and pecked her on the lips, "nice idea hun, but not very practical on a weekday morning."

"We have time, please, Tom we haven't done it in the morning for ages."

"That's because we both work and as I said, it's not practical." Pushing past her to get to the wardrobe he began assembling his clothes for the day.

"I want you, Tom please, I feel so horny, don't let a girl down, sometimes the rampant rabbit just isn't man enough for the job." Stretching out on the bed she gave him her best pout.

Whilst Tom had been showering she had blow-dried her hair, put on a tiny pair of black lace briefs and a short black lace slip. Touch of mascara, perfume and lip gloss and she knew she almost had him.

He laughed and started to grin. "You do look too gorgeous to ignore and after all, what's a girl to do if the rabbit can't cut it?"

"Exactly. Come here."

He sat down beside her on the bed and leant in to kiss her. She smelt and looked gorgeous and he remembered why he'd fallen for her all those years before. Stroking her breast he felt her nipple harden and he pulled the lace down to reach it with his mouth. She put her head back and moaned, "I want you inside me." His hand travelled down to the lace briefs and as he started to slowly pull the lace down she lifted her bottom off the bed and used her hands to quickly and unceremoniously free herself from them. He frowned.

"What's the hurry, I wanted to take them off you, we have time to play a bit surely?"

He traced his tongue down her stomach and parted her thighs with his hands. Gazing at her he smiled. "Best thing about doing this in the daylight... I get to look at you properly." He kissed her clitoris and moving down began to tease her opening with his tongue, circling and circling, tickling and teasing. "Stop teasing me...I want you so much please get inside me."

"Ok, hang on...just wait a second, I'm enjoying this." He went to slide two fingers inside her but found he couldn't easily enter her. She was a little dry and tense, not really ready, certainly not as ready as she claimed to be, she was usually soaked by the time he got to finger her. Withdrawing he licked one and slid it into her, "ooh that's so good, I'm coming… oh God…oh God." She shuddered and started to rock and thrust her hips against his hand. Curiously he studied her face as she appeared to orgasm.

"Fuck me, Tom fuck me please," she groaned, maneuvering herself to reach his now flaccid cock.

"What's wrong, you're not hard."

"Yeh and you weren't wet so I guess we're both liars, good performance though." He removed his fingers and turned away.

"What do you mean? I want you, Tom." She bent to take him in her mouth and she skillfully began to tease and work the head of his penis with her tongue. Against his wishes he began to harden. Suddenly an image of Lucy leaning over him in the front seat of the car shot into his consciousness. He jumped and Sophie thought he was about to come.

"Hang on. Wait until you're inside me." She lay back, legs open; she seductively began to stroke herself. He decided to call her bluff. "You go on top."

"Tom you know I don't like that. Come on I'm ready."

"You used to," she continued to work him with her other hand.

"I want you, Tom please."

He closed his eyes and entered her. He felt his erection struggling when her hands grabbed his arse and seemed to urge him further in. He wasn't going to come, he knew what this farce had been about, she hadn't felt horny, and she just needed his sperm. He knew if he opened his eyes to look at her he would lose his hard-on. He made a choice, and he chose to imagine he was with Lucy, her pussy, her hands, her mouth he bent to kiss, her breast he rubbed. He just prayed Sophie didn't speak, but she did.

"That's it...ooh that's so good."

"Shut the fuck up...don't make a sound unless you want me to stop."

Shocked Sophie stared at his face, eyes closed, deep in concentration and as he pumped his way to orgasm she knew with absolute certainty behind his eyelids he was with someone else. It occurred to her that she'd reached a new low; the really troubling thing was that she really didn't care.

Rolling off, he silently headed for his second shower of the day whilst Sophie did exactly what he knew she would. She swiveled round and, placing a pillow under her bottom she put her legs up on the wall.

Standing under the hot water he shook his head at his gullibility, about how easily he'd fallen for the flattery.

"What a bloody joke," he muttered. He had thought things had gotten better between them. He'd been wrong. Her agenda might be hidden behind, pleasantries, black lace and smiles but it was obviously still there.

* * *

"Well?" Kirsty called through the bathroom door? The door opened and Lucy thrust the plastic stick at her. She'd been crying again. Smiling Kirsty took the stick from her shaking hand.

"Based on how teary you are today I reckon it's positive."

"Yes it fucking is…oh, Kirst I am so screwed, how can this be happening to me?"

"That's not exactly the issue is it? What about the father? Does he know? Are you going to tell him?"

"I can't think about that right now, I really can't. I'm too shocked."

"You have to, you really have to. He's got to know and you've got to give him a chance to be involved."

"It's not that simple."

"Go on."

"He's married." Shock spread across Kirsty's face.

"What were you thinking? You stupid cow!"

"Thanks, that helps, I suppose I wasn't thinking if I'm honest, I cocked up ok?"

They made their way downstairs to the lounge and sat opposite each other.

"Who is it, Luce? Do I know him?"

"No. I used to work with him."

"That explains why you quit your job then?"

"Yeh, I really liked him, loved him a bit I guess. He's older, really good looking but most of all he took care of me, made me feel special. I started it, it was all me, not his fault."

"He could have said no you know, he didn't have to do it."

"Anyway he told me that it was a mistake and we couldn't sleep together anymore, and I couldn't bear to see him and not touch or kiss him, I wanted to be with him so badly so I just left."

"Such a bloody drama queen."

"That's not fair."

"Yes it is, you have a two second fling with a married man and 'cause he calls it off you walk out on a decent job when, quite frankly, you could do with the money."

"Stop being a bitch. I overreacted I get it ok?"

"Mum and dad can't afford to keep you and a baby you know."

"Ok, I said I get it. I've ruined my whole life and theirs too by the sound of it."

Lucy stood and walked to the window.

"I'll tell him. I'll have to won't I?"

"Yes."

"He'll hate me. What if he thinks I did this on purpose?"

"Did you?" Lucy spun round to face her sister, her face red with fury.

"Piss off."

"Just asking."

"Well don't."

"Are you gonna ask him to leave his wife?"

"Of course not. It's not about me it's about the baby and his responsibility."

"Just keep telling yourself that."

"You're being a cow."

Slowly Kirsty stood up and walked over to her sister.

"I'm sorry." She put her arms around her and as Lucy started to cry Kirsty remembered the joy of sharing the news of her pregnancy with Alex and found herself crying too.

CHAPTER 9

"Mate, I need a massive favor."

"Ok."

"Don't you wanna know what it is first?"

"What can it be that I need to think about it, whatever it is, you got it. You know that."

"Cheers, I really appreciate that."

"Go on then."

"Can I stop at yours for a bit. I think me and Soph need a bit of time apart. Well I do at least."

"Course you can that's fine, just bring your stuff over."

"Tonight ok?"

"Fine, I'll drop you a key down to your desk. I'll leave it in the top drawer."

"Thanks, I'm taking a half day to clear my stuff out so I'll be there when you get in."

"Well make sure my dinner's on the table; you do realize this makes you my bitch now."

"Fuck off."

Tom finished the call. He'd finally decided to do it, to leave, he felt some guilt but the overwhelming feeling was one of relief. Sitting in his car outside the house, plan in place he pulled out into the traffic and wondered if this would be the last time he'd makes this particular journey to work.

* * *

She opened the front door to silence. As usual she had arrived home first. She placed her handbag on the kitchen table and moved to fill the kettle. She kicked off her shoes and sat down. She looked at the clock; he'd be home soon so she'd better get upstairs. She removed the small, white pharmacy bag from her hand-bag and as she did she noticed the white envelope on the table. She'd obviously knocked it over when she put her bag down. It was Tom's writing and it was addressed to her.

Sophie,

I'm sorry but I can't live like this anymore. I'm moving in with Andy for a bit. We need some space. I hate that we keep hurting each other. I feel this is for the best. I'll be in touch.

Tom.

Throwing the letter down she ran to the lounge and slammed on the light, his laptop and i-pod were gone. Upstairs she threw open the wardrobe and was confronted by rows of empty hangers and shelves. His drawers, were, likewise empty with only the new boxers remaining.

In the bathroom she was met by huge gaps on the shelves where Tom's shaver, toothbrush, hair gel, deodorant and aftershave had sat.

She slumped onto the toilet lid and hung her head in her hands.

"You bastard...why now, after all this?" She eventually gave into the tears that started to come.

Entering the newly painted kitchen her eyes fell on the small, white bag sticking out of her handbag. She picked it up and slid out the pregnancy test. The irony of the situation was not lost on her as she grinned ruefully, "typical, I could find out I'm pregnant the day my husband leaves me because he can't cope with the fact I can't get pregnant. Great timing huh?"

She put the test on the table and turned to make the coffee. Absently she placed two cups next to the kettle before she realized and pushed one out of the way.

She would drink her coffee, calm down and then head upstairs, she had to know, one way or the other. She was a mixture of excitement and fear. All the time the test remained on the table she could keep the hope alive. The moment the test said 'not pregnant' her heart would break all over again. To hope and not know was better than to face the gut wrenching disappointment. As the coffee reached her lips she screwed up her face. "Shit...that smells awful." Taking another strong sniff she grimaced, slammed the cup down and lunged for the sink, vomiting.

She wiped her mouth and gave a nervous giggle. 'I've never had that reaction to coffee before' she thought and smiled, 'I used to love coffee.'

Knowing she couldn't put it off any longer she picked up the kit and went upstairs.

* * *

Andy's apartment was huge. He'd lost both parents to a car crash fifteen years earlier and had inherited a large sum from their estates. Having invested wisely he was now in the fortunate position of working because he wanted to and it amused him not because he needed to.

Standing in front of the full length windows Tom gazed out at the city. His suitcases stood behind him, lost in the huge second bedroom. The super-kingsize bed sat against one wall with floor to ceiling wardrobes filling the adjacent wall. The door to the en-suite wet-room opened to the right and a forty-two inch flat screen plasma TV sat opposite the bed. It was stunning, but all Tom felt was numb. Looking west he imagined Sophie coming home, opening the letter and crying. Even now he wasn't sure if he'd done the right thing. He knew he couldn't keep hurting her but by leaving he had probably hurt her more.

He unpacked and only managed to use half the wardrobe space available. He stashed his cases in the empty side. The city lights looked amazing. He heard the front door open.

"Hi mate. Settled in ok?"

"Yeh good thanks."

Andy hung his coat up and headed for the kitchen area of the large open plan living space. Flicking on the TV he reached to pour two large whiskeys.

"Here you go."

"Cheers."

"Reckon you need it more than me today. What did she say when you left?"

"No idea, I packed up while she was at work and left her a note."

"What?"

"I just couldn't face another slagging match, I'm completely knackered mate, really. I know it's a cowardly thing to do but once I'd decided to go I just wanted to be away from her." Andy stared at Tom for several seconds before walking past him towards the lounge. Tom followed sheepishly. Andy was always brutally honest but it was often hard to hear.

They both sat on opposite ends of the corner unit staring at the TV in silence.

"Are you gonna ring her?"

"Sometime, but not yet. I can't."

"I do understand you know, you think I don't but I do and more importantly, I'm on your side no matter what ok?"

Tom let out a huge sigh and allowed himself a smile.

"Thank fuck for that."

"Sorry for giving you a hard time, that wasn't fair; I just speak before I think sometimes."

"No mate you just say what needs to be said."

They both grinned and knocked back their drinks.

"Erm...there is something else." Andy rose to refill their glasses.

"Go on."

"I'm really sorry but I have plans tonight, long-standing plans with someone who landed today and flies out of Heathrow again tomorrow. I feel bad and I'll happily cancel if you want me to."

"No you won't you tart." Tom grinned.

"No of course not but I had to offer."

"Go and get laid Jones, just don't brag about it to me."

"I won't, it's a 'he' this time so I won't bore you with the details, might put you off your breakfast."

"Fair enough. I don't mind hearing about the stewardesses but the stewards you can keep to yourself."

"Deal."

Andy had been bi-sexual for as long as he could remember. He was always discreet and never let his sexual preferences encroach on his work or his friendships. Vehemently single he shagged his way around the city with a great deal of style and always with a condom.

He heard Andy's shower start and finish and realized he'd been staring at the TV without taking anything of the programme on board. After twenty more minutes Andy emerged from his room in a cloud of Armani and even Tom could appreciate how fantastic he looked.

"Looking good mate."

"Cheers."

Sitting next to him Andy turned to face him, "seriously, I feel really bad about leaving you alone like this, for Christ's sake your marriage just broke up...I'm staying, that's it." Andy rose and started to remove his jacket and kick off his shoes. Tom put his hands up in protest.

"Oy stop it tit-head, put those back on and listen. To be honest I'd be shit company and I could do with a couple of hours alone to sort my head, really. That's the truth. If you were here I'd feel obliged to make conversation and be sociable and that's the last thing I want to be right now so go and get laid and don't worry about me."

"You really sure?"

"YES, piss off."

"Ok then, see ya."

"Bye."

The door slammed and Tom suddenly felt very alone. He'd left his wife, he'd left his home, his car belonged to the dealership. It occurred to him how little he'd achieved in thirty-eight years. He felt his eyes fill with tears and knew this was just self-pity and maybe a bit of shock.

Wiping his face with his hand he stood and refilled his glass. He felt pissed but didn't care. He'd ordered a pizza and had just settled on the huge sofa with the scotch when his phone received a text.

'We need to talk. I'm pregnant.'

CHAPTER 10

As the taxi dropped him off he felt the effects of the scotch and wished he'd had time to eat the pizza. He went in and saw her sitting in the corner. He smiled although his hands were shaking.

"Can I get you a drink?"

"Just bitter lemon please."

She looked so young.

He returned with the drinks and sat down opposite her. She was staring at the beer-mat in her hands twisting it nervously. He reached forward and took it from her, laying it on the table, he then reached forward and took her chin and tilted her face towards him.

"Talk to me, Luce" he said softly.

"I don't know what to say." Her eyes started to brim with tears.

"Yes you do. You're pregnant and it's mine."

"That's pretty much it really."

"Ok." He took her hand.

"What do you want to do?"

"I'm having it."

"Are you sure?"

"Yes definitely, my sister had to have an abortion because of severe birth defects and the guilt nearly killed her, she felt so bad. I'm not getting rid of it that's final and if you don't like it then that's fine I'll manage on my own." She looked so young and yet so strong and determined. He grinned at her.

"I get it, no abortion, it's ok. Do you know how scary you are when you're angry?"

She burst out laughing.

He placed a hand on her knee. "Sexy too."

"Behave yourself, Tom this is important."

"I know it is but I just wanted to tell you I've missed you every day since you got out of the car and disappeared, I've thought about you a lot and for what it's worth I'm sorry for what I said that day. I was wrong."

"What does that mean?"

"I left Sophie today, I missed you and it wasn't working out anymore, things had been bad for a while but I realized I couldn't be with her when we wanted different things and every time I touched her all I could see was you."

"You left her today?"

"Yeh."

"Where are you living then?"

"I'm stopping with Andy for a bit."

"What about if she wants to try again?"

"It doesn't matter."

"She's your wife."

"And I want you...both of you."

He took both her hands in his and leaning forward he kissed her softly.

"You're really gonna be a part of this?"

"Definitely."

She threw her arms around his neck and they hugged and as she did he couldn't help but wonder if he'd just made another huge mistake.

"I never imagined you'd say that, never. It's more than I ever hoped for. Tom you need to know I think I love you."

For a second he hesitated and her face fell. He felt a wave of guilt wash over him, and in that split second the options ran through his mind, if he didn't say it he would hurt her and if he did he would've lied. He made his choice.

"I think I love you too."

She beamed. "So what now?"

"Let's go back to Andy's we can talk in peace then."

"Are you sure he won't mind?"

"He's out and believe me, even if he wasn't that place is big enough to have a blazing row at one end and he wouldn't hear you at the other."

They left the pub and decided to walk. It was cold and fresh and Tom wrapped his arm around her shoulders.

"Need to take care of yourself now."

"I'm fine."

"Let's keep it that way shall we?"

"That's what I love about you; you make me feel so special, so wanted, so cared for."

He stopped and turned to face her.

"Good, that's how you should be treated, you are special and you are gorgeous and I'm hard just being here with you. You amaze me."

They kissed and as he opened his overcoat she slipped her arms inside and around his waist. He was straining against his flies and as she began rubbing him through the fabric he let out a deep guttural moan. His hand moved up her thigh and quickly found her little lacy knickers. She closed her eyes.

Slipping his finger between the lace and her skin she gently bit his lip and dipped her tongue into his mouth hungrily. "Come over here," he whispered.

He took her hand and led her down a narrow alley that led to the back gardens of the houses in the next road. It was dark and quiet and once in the shadows he felt for her nipple through her clothes, feeling it harden under his touch he slid his hand lower and up under her skirt, feeling for the edge of her lace knickers. She was wet as he traced the silky, moist folds of her and as they kissed she began to rub him harder through his trousers. "We need some privacy, come on."

Taking her hand he stepped into the busy street and hailed the nearest cab and once in the dark, semi-private backseat he reached for her again.

During the short ten minute journey he removed her pants and tucked them in his coat pocket, "you won't need those again tonight." She giggled as she climbed on top of him and began to rub herself against his swollen crotch.

The cabbie, a driver of many years experience glimpsed Tom in the mirror, their eyes met and as Tom smiled the driver winked and nodded appreciatively. As they clambered from the backseat Tom paid the £15 fare with a £50 note without waiting for the change.

* * *

He opened the door to Andy's apartment and as she stepped into the hallway Lucy gasped. "Oh my God, you weren't joking were you? This place is huge."

"It's gorgeous isn't it?"

She ran to the huge windows and gazed out at the city. "What a view."

"I couldn't agree more but I think it's slightly overdressed." She spun round looking confused. "What?"

"You, I'd rather look at you but you're a little overdressed for my liking."

"Easy tiger."

"You just get yourself over here."

They met in the middle of the room and without a word he began to undress her very slowly.

As he removed each garment he kissed the exposed flesh until only her bra remained. He turned her round and undid the bra and let it fall to the floor amongst her other clothes. Reaching round her he took the weight of her breasts in his hands. "Where did these come from?"

He spun her to face him and gazed longingly at her. "It's because I'm pregnant numb-nuts," she told him laughing.

"They were beautiful before and I wouldn't have changed anything about you, but shit, they're amazing, they're huge."

"Yeh I know, I get it, I've got big tits now." She slapped his arm playfully.

Tweaking her nipple with one hand he bent to suck the other. Her breasts were bigger and heavier and the nipples seemed darker, he was enthralled with the changes.

She let out a deep sigh, "I have missed you so much."

He took her hand and led her into his bedroom. "Wow what a room, is this where you're sleeping?"

"No, it's where *we're* sleeping." They grinned at each other.

"Works for me," and she jumped up onto the enormous bed.

He climbed on top of her and placed his hand on her thighs.

"Is it safe to do it? For the baby I mean?"

The concern in his eyes touched her heart. Reaching up to stroke his face she nodded, "as long as you're gentle it's fine."

"Open up for me gorgeous, I wanna look at you."

Spreading her legs he gazed at her moist, glistening, pink folds. "You are so beautiful and you never get embarrassed do you? I love looking at you."

"And I love you looking at me. Why should I be embarrassed? We're having a baby together, I can't worry about being shy in front of you, by the time I have this baby the world and his wife will have had a look."

He smiled and gently began to stroke her. Gradually he worked his fingers into every fold and as she gave herself over to his touch he slowly brought her closer and closer. He couldn't have been more gentle or patient. She was so wet and he desperately wanted to finger her but he just rubbed the opening and teased her clitoris with his other hand. She writhed and thrashed on the bed as her climax approached. He watched as her body responded to his touch, the flush on her breasts, the swelling of her lips as she bit them, her sexy little nub growing against his fingers. He watched her start to pulsate and as she came he slid two fingers into her and she bore down on them as he rubbed her over and over until the orgasm subsided. She was soaked and he was struggling to control his own orgasm despite his trousers remaining done up. "I want you inside me."

"Are you sure it's ok?"

"Honestly." She reached over and helped him out of his clothes. Pushing him onto his back she mounted him and eased onto his waiting cock.

"Shit, that's fantastic." He closed his eyes.

She moved instinctive, and he took the opportunity to look at her. Yes, her breasts were bigger but her hips seemed slightly wider and her normally flat stomach looked a little rounder too. She looked sexier, more womanly. He felt the climax approaching, he gripped her hips and she opened her eyes and smiled at him. She had one hand between her legs and was rubbing herself; he slid his fingers down to take over. Within seconds she was coming furiously again, and he let himself come with her.

* * *

By the time Andy arrived home at about three am Tom had moved Lucy's clothes into the bedroom and sent a quick text to warn Andy that he had another guest.

At ten he awoke to find Lucy looking down at him smiling. They hadn't drawn the blinds the night before and the city was enjoying a sunny, spring Saturday.

"Hi."

"Hi."

"You ok?"

"Yeh. I was sick earlier though."

"Oh shit. You ok?" His face was full of concern until he saw her smile. "Oh I get it, morning sickness right?"

"It doesn't happen very often now; I'm hopefully coming to the end of it."

"I think I have some questions I need to ask you before we go on much further."

"Oh?"

He pushed himself up and arranged the pillows so they were facing each other. "How old are you? What's your surname? When's the baby due? Have you seen a doctor yet? Erm think that's it for now. Hang on. Do you parents know and if so do they know about me?"

"Ok well I'm twenty two, its Millson. I'm due 28th of October. I have seen the GP and I'm due to see the midwife this week and my twelve week scan's next week. No and no. Is that it?"

"Shit, your dad's gonna freak at the age thing you know."

"Probably."

"That's not helping."

She laughed. "Tough." They both jumped as Andy knocked on the door.

"Come in mate," Tom called.

As he entered the room carrying a tray with coffee, cups and toast he stopped dead in his tracks. Stiffening he placed the tray on the dresser and turned to leave. "Can I have a word please, Tom?"

Fumbling for his robe he quickly followed Andy into the kitchen pulling the door shut behind him.

"I thought it was gonna be Sophie, that you'd patched things up, that you'd got back together but you leave your wife and the same day you're shagging your little bit on the side all over again. What the fuck are you doing?" Andy was scarlet with rage. Tom noticed his knuckles were white as he gripped the edge of the worktop.

Tom slammed his hand down on to the granite.

"Will you shut up and stop assuming the worst for one fucking minute?"

Taking a deep breath he continued.

"I tried to make it work with Sophie but every time I touched her I missed Lucy, every time we made love it was Lucy I saw, Lucy I wanted and FYI she text me something rather important and life changing which is why I went to meet her and talk. I didn't leave Sophie just because things were wrong between us I left because

I missed Lucy and it felt wrong being without her." His voice dropped. "She's pregnant."

Andy's head shot up. "You bloody idiot, as midlife crises go this is monumental."

"Fuck off."

"You think you're the father do you? Yeh right, you just happen to be earning more than the other little scrotes she's probably fucked since you."

They both heard the front door slam.

"You bastard. LUCE...LUCE!"

Tom chased after her onto the landing just as the lift arrived. He managed to stop the doors before they closed. She'd been crying.

He took her in his arms and she buried her face into his shoulder. He stroked her hair until she calmed.

"Everyone will think I'm a gold-digger or a stupid little slut who got knocked-up on purpose."

"Who cares?"

"He's your friend-your best friend, and he hates me already."

"Come back inside please, he needs to get to know you that's all."

Reluctantly she followed him into the flat.

Andy stood at the breakfast bar looking ashamed.

CHAPTER 11

She opened her eyes and rolled over, smiling. She stroked her as yet still flat stomach. Sitting up she felt the wave of nausea break over her. She'd had to get up to wee twice in the night and each time she felt sure she'd see the tell-tale blood but with every minute the reality of her pregnancy became more real.

Taking a sip of water she picked up her lap-top and sitting cross-legged on her bed she switched it on. Within minutes she'd calculated her due date and ordered several pregnancy ad-vice books. Giggling to herself she stuffed a pil-low inside her dressing-gown as she paraded in front of the full length mirror. She caressed her 'pretend' bump and grinned. It was really hap-pening, finally.

* * *

"Lucy I'm sorry I was so rude, I just don't want Tom getting screwed over that's all. I don't know you or anything about you, all I know is that he cheated on his wife of ten years with a girl sixteen years his junior in the boiler-room during his lunch break who now claims to be having his baby. Quite frankly it's like a soap opera and it's a little hard to swallow. He might buy it cause he's horny as hell for you but not me, I'm gonna need a lot more convincing. Ok?"

She sat bolt upright on the sofa, staring into the distance.

"That's fine, Andy here goes. I fell for Tom the first night he picked me up at the bus-stop, he *was* horny as hell and couldn't take his eyes off me but I knew he was married so I didn't do anything except enjoy his company, I was flattered. That day he threatened Lee I knew I wanted him. That simple. I didn't plan to sleep with him just a quick fumble maybe but he just went for it and I was swept away. I thought I was safe, I was on the pill but a couple of weeks before when I'd been away on a hen weekend I'd forgotten to take my pills with me. I just restarted them when I got home and assumed I'd be ok. When I didn't come on I worked it out and couldn't believe I'd been so stupid. I didn't mean to get pregnant. Please, I have no job, I live with my parents. Not ideal."

"So Tom's quite a catch then really?"

"Andy that's enough." Tom stood up.

"I will have every DNA test known to man I will ask the midwife to work out the date of conception and you can confirm the date with when we shagged if you like. It's his, I swear. What can I say to convince you?"

Tom sat back down and took her hand, it was shaking.

"You don't have to say anything," he reassured her.

"Obviously I do."

"Andy tell her please, if you're my friend please tell her you believe her."

Tom's eyes met Andy's and Andy looked away.

"Ok fine, whatever you say. It's none of my business is it?"

"Only in as much as you're like a brother to me and I don't want to fall out with you but I won't have Lucy upset anymore. Regardless of what you think she's still pregnant and she doesn't need the stress."

"Agreed."

Andy rose and disappeared into the kitchen.

"Tea, coffee, or something stronger? Lucy?"

"I can't face tea or coffee at the moment and of course I can't drink either, as you're no doubt aware, so water will be fine thanks." She attempted a smile.

"I'm so sorry," Tom whispered into her ear.

He held her as she stared out over the city holding back the tears.

* * *

Tom pulled up outside Lucy's house to drop her off, they'd agreed that he would tell Sophie and she would tell her parents. Still reeling from Andy's reaction they felt it best to tell their respective stories alone and meet up later.

Lucy opened the front door and was met by the usual cacophony of the television blaring, her parents chatting, and the clattering of pans from the kitchen. Dinner smelt good but she felt nauseous again and wasn't sure if it was partly fear.

Walking into the kitchen-diner she sat down heavily at the table. She reached for the remote control and muted the TV.

"Oy I was watching that," her dad moaned.

"No you weren't you were talking to mum, anyway I want you both to sit down I need to talk to you." Her parents exchanged concerned looks.

"Ok, what is it?" Lucy looked at her hands; she couldn't meet her parent's eyes.

"I have some news, it's going to shock and probably upset you but I hope as you get used to the idea you'll be happy for me."

"Oh my God you're going round the world travelling aren't you?"

Her mother's hands flew to her mouth. "Please don't go, Luce; it's dangerous for girls away from home…"

Looking up she interrupted. "Mum I'm pregnant."

For several moments there was silence. Her father slammed the flat of his hand against the table before standing up and walking to the kitchen to get a beer, slamming the fridge door in the process.

Her mother just stared at her, disappointment in her eyes.

"You're keeping it aren't you? You wouldn't have told us otherwise."

"Yes I'm keeping it and the father's supporting me too."

"Who is it? Do we know him?"

"It's someone from work; he's a bit older than me."

"What's 'a bit'?" her father growled as he sat back down.

"He's…well…he's thirty-eight."

"FUCKING HELL!!" Her father exploded. "He's old enough to be your father, dirty bastard; you wait till I get hold of him."

"Stop it," her mother said softly placing a hand over her father's clenched fist.

"This is Lucy we're talking about. We have to have a little trust and faith, just listen before you go off on one. Go on, Luce." She smiled at her daughter encouragingly.

"Ok, well we met at work and one thing led to another, I thought I was safe but I forgot to take my pills when I went away for Phoebe's hen weekend so that's how it happened."

"When's it due?"

"End of October, the 28th"

"Dear God that makes you what...nearly three months gone? How could you keep it from me? Does Kirsty know?"

Her mother's eyes filled with tears.

"Yes."

Her father raised his head and studied her face. "He's married isn't he?"

Lucy looked away.

"Lucy, tells me he isn't, please?" Her mother implored.

Lucy lowered her head and stared at her hands. "He's separated actually."

"Did he leave his wife for you though? Answer me," he growled.

"He left because of me but before he knew I was pregnant, he left because he loves me not because he felt responsible."

"You silly little girl."

Her father stormed from the room.

"Dad..."

"Leave him, he's upset, he's got to get his head around it first, you're his little girl, and after what's just happened with Kirsty he's still very raw."

"It'll be ok mum, I promise, he really loves me, honestly."

"Then why has he left you to tell us on your own?"

"I told him to, I knew you'd react like this and so did he, he's not scared. Actually he's gone to tell his wife."

"Oh dear God, that poor woman."

"Mum she's a complete bitch...she was so obsessed with having a baby she drove him mad, I suppose that's good though otherwise we wouldn't have found each other."

"Will you listen to yourself; I don't even know you anymore. You stupid child, what have you done, Lucy what the hell have you done?"

Her mother stood up and silently left the room, Lucy knew she was crying.

"Mum...MUM..." Her mother disappeared upstairs and slammed the bedroom door.

"Shit." Lucy muttered as she walked over to the cooker and began turning the rings off under the pans on the hob. She assumed after her parent's reaction they wouldn't feel much like eating tonight.

She grabbed her coat and left, softly closing the front door behind her.

* * *

He felt the keys in his pocket but opted to use the bell instead. As the door opened Sophie gasped.

"Tom, I wasn't expecting you, why didn't you use your key? Come in."

Without waiting for him she turned and walked down the hall to the kitchen. As he entered he heard the kettle start to boil. "Sit down, I was going to say 'make yourself at home'." He forced a smile and sat at the table.

"It's good of you to see me? How are you?"

"Me, I'm fine thanks, you?"

"Erm...ok...I need to talk to you, there's something I wanted you to hear from me not anyone else."

"Coffee? Tea?"

"No, thanks. Soph, please sit down, this is important and it's not going to be easy."

He noticed her hand shaking as she pulled out the dining chair opposite him. "Ok, go for it."

He sighed and reached for her hands, looking into her eyes he began. "I cheated on you before I left, with someone I met at work; the thing is... she's pregnant."

Instantly Sophie pulled her hands from his, she stood with such ferocity that the chair fell backwards.

"You bastard...YOU PIECE OF SHIT!!!"

"I know I'm so, so, sorry."

"YOU ALWAYS FUCKING ARE. GET OUT, JUST GO."

"Sophie, please, let me explain, it was an accident." Choking back a sob she pointed towards the front door.

"Please leave me some dignity and go."

"No, I won't leave you like this," and stepping forward he took her in his arms.

Instantly she stiffened but as he refused to loosen his grip she gradually melted into his arms, weeping. Silently he stroked her hair until she calmed. With alarming clarity the thought occurred to him that it felt completely natural to hold this woman, it wasn't about sex or marriage or babies it was a decade of understanding and friendship. He knew at that very moment that if she asked him to stay, he would.

Reaching down to take her chin he tilted her tear-stained face up to meet his and softly kissed her on the mouth, as she responded their tongues met. His hand began to stroke her cheek and as he ran a finger down her neck towards her breast his mobile phone rang.

"I'd better get that."

"Don't, Tom please."

He bent to kiss her again and she pressed her body against his.

"I'll just see who it is, I won't answer it." Reaching into his pocket to withdraw the phone he paled as he looked at the caller ID.

"It's her isn't it? How ironic, now it appears that *I'm* the other woman." She laughed bitterly.

"It doesn't matter come here." He reached for her but she pushed him away.

"She's the mother of your child...is that how little you care?"

He ran his fingers through his hair, she thought he looked tired. "It's not as simple as that."

"Oh, Tom what a mess, you'd better go. I need to think."

"I don't want to leave. I didn't realize until I got here how much I miss you."

"Pity you didn't think of that before you fathered a bastard child with someone else then." She glowered.

"We could try again...please."

For a split second she considered telling him about the baby. If she told him would he stay and if he did would he be staying for her or the child and what about the other baby, did she really want to be with a man who had raped her, cheated, fathered a baby with another woman? She imagined Christmases with both children sharing their father, a constant memory of his betrayal and she knew her decision was made.

"Tom, please go."

CHAPTER 12

Sitting in the car he listened to her voicemail. It had been a disaster, her parents had taken the news really badly and she was crying, waiting at the bus-station to be picked up.

He saw her on the corner and pulled over. Climbing into the car she fell into his arms sobbing. "It was awful, they hate me."

"No they don't they're disappointed, shocked that's all, give them time. It'll be ok, I promise." He held her gently.

"My dad wants to kill you."

Tom laughed.

"Don't laugh. He really does, he's furious, I don't know if it's the age thing or being married that did it."

"Oh shit, you told 'em that too?"

Tom pulled away and looked Lucy in the eye. "Was that wise?"

"No point in drip feeding 'em the news, better they be mad all at once."

"Maybe you're right. Let's go, I need a drink."

He pulled out into the traffic and headed for Andy's.

* * *

Sophie stood in the middle of the kitchen leaning against the worktop hugging herself, shocked and stunned. Torn between the memory of how good it had been to have Tom hold her and how he'd completely destroyed everything by getting someone else pregnant.

She tenderly stroked her stomach, imagining sharing her child with this other woman, dropping it off at weekends, birthdays, Christmases, sitting with them at school plays. If he was going to be with someone else then her child would have a stepmother and half brother or sister. The ripples would continue to affect her life for years. He'd spoiled everything.

* * *

As they opened the door Tom and Lucy were met by the sight of two naked figures on the sofa. Frozen in the doorway for several seconds, too shocked to move or look away they realized it was Andy and an unknown man. Andy was spread-eagled on the sofa whilst the other man's head was buried in his groin. Andy was moaning and clutching his partners hair as his eyes opened and instantly met Tom's. His expression showed no flicker of shame or embarrassment and as he gazed at Tom he continued to moan and pant until he came into his partner's mouth, without breaking eye contact.

Lucy hurried into the bedroom and slammed the door as Tom cleared his throat. The stranger stood, unashamedly wiping his mouth. Andy stood up and gesturing towards his partner said, "didn't expect you back so soon, this is Mike."

Mike waved casually as he proceeded to retrieve his clothes from around the room.

"Hi Mike. Andy. Sorry we disturbed you."

"No worries mate, I'm good. You didn't disturb us at all, well no more than me coming home disturbed your little fuck-fest the other night."

Tom strode across the room, "is that what this is about? You're making a point?!"

"No actually I'm getting laid, in *my* apartment, is there a problem?"

"No problem at all, we'll just get our things and be out of your way. Luce, we're leaving hun, get your stuff," he called as he headed for the bedroom.

Andy hurried after him, and grabbed Tom's arm. "Mate, stop. I'm sorry, I was being a shit, please don't go. You stay as long as you want. Really."

"What about Lucy?"

"Of course, both of you. I'm just pissed and forgot you were due back, I'm sorry."

Turning towards the large picture window and the man in his underpants he called, "Mike... pour some drinks please, I'll meet you in the shower yeh?"

"How did it go with Soph?"

"It was awful, she broke down. I'm such a dick, I feel like shit."

"You're not a dick, you just screwed up, just let everyone get used to the idea eh? Look how I was at first, totally freaked but I'm ok with it now."

"Really?"

"Really."

Tom threw his arms round his best friend and hugged him. Feeling tears threatening he rubbed his eyes self-consciously. "And' you're the only friend I've got right now, I need your support on this I really do, please."

"I'll always be here for you mate, rape, bastard children, separation, you name it I'll be there no worries."

They grinned at each other and hugged again.

"Come on you twat, let's have a drink."

Andy led Tom to the kitchen where Mike waited with three large scotches. All three downed them instantly. "Well, Mike nice to meet you, if a tad embarrassing." Tom extended his right hand.

"Nice to meet you too, I've heard a lot about you," Mike shook hands grinning.

"Shut up, Mike," Andy snapped. "Just don't, ok?"

"What's this?" Tom looked from one to the other, curious.

"It's nothing really; I said I'd meet you in the shower, Mike...Please."

"Ok babe, as you wish." Mike kissed Andy on the lips and wandered off to Andy's bedroom.

"Er...did I miss something?"

"No why?"

"What's going on mate?"

"I'm just going for a shower; help yourself to another drink ok?"

"Andy...ANDY what's going on?" But the bedroom door closed on his question.

CHAPTER 13

"You didn't tell me Andy was gay. That was embarrassing and if I'm honest, very sexy." She put her hand over her mouth and giggled.

"He's bi-sexual actually. I don't know about sexy but it was embarrassing that's for sure."

He plopped down on the bed next to her and pulling off her shoes he began to rub her feet. "Oooh that's amazing...mmm love it."

He laughed, "you're easily pleased, wait till I move up a bit."

"Promises promises."

"That bloke Mike, Andy's 'friend'" he said drawing parenthesis is the air with his fingers.

"Yes...nice arse."

"Behave yourself...He implied that Andy had mentioned me in some way before, he said he'd heard a lot about me."

"Yeh, that's natural, you're like brothers... and?"

"Well Andy got arsy with him and basically couldn't get him out of the room fast enough."

"That's good...mmm...what, oh yeh, that is weird. What do you think Andy'd said about you?"

"No idea."

His hand left her foot and began to massage her calf and then her thigh. "Mmm that's lovely, don't stop...oooh yeah that's nice. I could do with a proper massage, I feel awful after telling mum and dad, so stressed."

"Ok strip off then and I'll give you the massage of your life," he said grinning, rubbing his hands together.

"Really? We're gonna make love right?"

"Maybe, but that'll be afterwards ok?"

"Ok."

She shuffled off the bed and emerged from the bathroom minutes later wrapped in a bath sheet. "Lay down...oh can you lay face down when you're pregnant?"

"At eleven weeks it's fine." She smiled at his concern. Hopping off the bed he disappeared into the bathroom.

"Ok then...I'll be two secs."

He returned wearing a robe and carrying some massage oil.

Slowly and gently he began at her feet and worked his way up her calves and thighs. The scent of white musk enveloped them as he started to knead her buttocks.

"Oh my God that feels incredible," she growled. "Don't stop."

He laughed, "it's not what you think you know, this is really a massage not foreplay."

"Yeh right."

"It's true. Just wait."

He poured more oil and moved up to her back and shoulders, skillfully working out the stress from the day. Although he was fully aroused he took great care to hide his hard-on from view.

"I'm so relaxed I feel like I'm half asleep." Her eyes were closed and her voice was sluggish.

"Flip over then sleepy."

As she turned onto her back she lay before him naked, spreading her thighs she raised her arms above her head and attempted to pull him down for a kiss. "No you don't, you have to wait."

"You're a pussy tease."

"I know."

With the greatest care he soothed her hands, arms and shoulders; working the oil into every inch of her skin, as he worked down her chest he avoided her breasts despite the fact that the site of her pert nipples was driving him insane with lust.

As he approached her stomach he simply softly kissed her between her belly button and her tuft of soft pubic hair.

"Hey don't stop, touch me please."

"That's it madam, that's your massage. How do you feel?"

"Amazing but horny and frustrated." Placing his hands between her thighs he smiled.

"All relaxed and ready to play now then?"

Instantly she spread her legs and bent her knees. "You forgot to massage my perineum."

"Your what?"

"To help with childbirth, here I'll show you."

She took the small hand-mirror from the bedside cabinet and placed it between her legs where they could both see her glistening and pink. As she placed her fingers on her perineum, she began to circle, gently massaging the area.

"I think, as the father that should be my responsibility don't you?" He smirked. "It's a tough job but I'll give it a go, here lift up."

As he lifted her bottom he placed a pillow underneath, "that's better, lets me see what I'm doing."

Grinning she wriggled until he was kneeling between her thighs. "Ok, let's have a go then." She laughed.

"You're mad."

"And you're kinky...works for me...I want you so much you have no idea."

He worked his fingers around the opening and down towards her arse, gently massaging and rubbing the area.

"Oh fuck, you are so wet." He bent to lick her.

Looking up he took a deep breath. "Luce, you trust me right?"

"Course."

"Ok, relax, I'm not gonna hurt you ok?"

"Ok."

He reached for the lube they kept in the drawer and applied it to his left hand and gently started to work a finger into her anus. "Whoa... stop, no way."

"You said you trusted me."

"I do, but I don't take it up the arse."

"Shush. Ok, ok. I won't do anything you don't like. Honestly." He moved his hand and felt her relax.

He continued to work a finger around her pussy, careful to avoid penetrating her, whilst needing her buttocks.

As he worked his fingers slowly round and round he felt her relax. Carefully he slipped two fingers of his right hand into her. She was so wet he gasped. Gently he maneuvered his fingers around in her warm, wet opening. She was amazingly tight and hot but he felt her gradually open up.

Her head was thrown back and her breathing was coming in gasps and pants.

"Is that good?"

"Oh God yeh, that feels amazing...don't stop."

As he watched she brought her hand down and started to rub her clitoris. "Mmm you're gorgeous," he murmured. He removed a finger from her and guided one of hers in to join his. Their fingers moved together inside her and as her climax built he flicked her clitoris in rhythm with her hips.

As she came he removed his fingers and slid into her dripping wet pussy.

She gasped and her eyes flew open, "oh shit, that's amazing; take me, oh God, that's it, that's it."

He held on as long as he could and then erupted into her, driving his cock deep into her. As he looked down she was smiling. "That was amazing. Fancy a shower?"

"I love you, Tom."

"Me too."

"Really?"

"Of course."

* * *

The hot water cascaded down Mike's body as Andy soaped his buttocks, penis and balls.

"That's him isn't it? The one, your unrequited love?"

"Shut up," Andy growled.

"It is...the straight one. He's cute."

Taking Mike's cock roughly in his hand Andy bent to take it into his mouth. He worked the end with his tongue as he moved one hand gently massaging the balls, whilst the other worked up and down the slippery shaft using the warm water to smooth the skin. Mike groaned.

As he moved faster Mike grabbed his hair and pushed himself into Andy's mouth. Shuddering he came into Andy's mouth and all over his chest. "Oh, that was gorgeous." Andy stood and licked Mike's nipples before kissing him deeply. "Do I taste of you?"

"Actually you do you kinky bastard."

Mike laughed. Tenderly he took Andy's face in his hands and looked into his eyes. "It *is* him isn't it? I won't tell you know, it's ok."

Andy stared at Mike, "yes it's him, he's a fucking mess, left his wife, knocked up some little slag, a complete fucking disaster, who does he run to? Good old Andy, pity he brought her with him though."

They turned off the water and wrapped in two huge towels they fell on the bed.

"Maybe we should ask them to join in, you could do him, and I'll do her?"

"That would be funny if it wasn't so tragic."

Mike suddenly sat up and turned to face Andy. "Come to New York with me, just for a few weeks, it'll be great, please. Give yourself some space from those two."

"I can't."

"Why not? Leave that shitty job, you don't need it...come and stop with me." He rose from the bed and wandered to the window. It was true he didn't need the job and he could easily afford a break. Could he bear to leave Tom with everything that was going on? Mike stood behind him and put his arms around Andy's waist. They'd been seeing each other casually for about two years and both really enjoyed their time together. For a second Andy wondered if he and Mike could be a proper couple, and instantly dismissed the idea, he loved Tom had been in love with him for years, even though he knew that Tom was straight and he had no chance he couldn't help how he felt. He laid his forehead against the cool glass. It was starting to rain. Sliding the patio doors open he walked onto the balcony and stood naked in the rain with his face turned towards the sky.

"Babe?"

Turning to face him Andy smiled, "let's do it."

"Really?"

"Yeh really."

Mike fell into his arms and kissed him deeply and for once Andy pushed Tom from his mind and enjoyed the kiss for what it was.

CHAPTER 14

Tom,
I'm going to New York with Mike for a few weeks, just a short break that's all. Give you two sometime together. Look after the place for me. I'll be in touch when I get there. Sorry I've been such a shit, I hope it works out for you and Lucy.
Good luck mate.
Andy.

"Shit." He stared at the note in his hand.

Lucy wandered from the bedroom to put the kettle on. "What's the matter?"

"Andy's gone away for a few weeks, to New York. With Mike apparently."

"What? He's gone without saying goodbye, just like that? What about his job?"

"Don't think he gives a shit to be honest."

"Do we have to leave then?"

"No he's told us to look after the place for him."

"Oh my God. That's incredible."

She ran to him and hugged him.

"*I* still have to go to work you know."

"I know but isn't it great to have this place to ourselves for a bit?"

"Yes, and he apologized for being a shit too."

"Really?"

"Yeh."

"I guess it's just 'cause he cares so much for you, you said you were like brothers, especially since his parents died."

"True, but I wonder if he cares too much."

"How is that possible?" She moved back to the kitchen and continued to make breakfast. Following her he leant against the worktop and gazed absently at the floor.

"Although he's never shown me that side of himself until yesterday I always felt if I'd have given him any encouragement he'd have been into my pants in a flash, nothing really, just a feeling. Probably my imagination."

"Well, Mr Wilkes, you are gorgeous," smiling she kissed him on the cheek.

"Seriously, when we walked in yesterday he stared at me like he was challenging me to say something or break them up...it was weird."

"Maybe he's in love with you? That would explain his attitude towards me."

"No way! We've been mates for years, we've talked about women, sex, everything except him sleeping with blokes, he's told me all about the girls he's shagged. We've been really pissed and even slept in the same bed but he's never, and I mean never once touched me or hinted at anything other than friendship."

"Why do you feel like he'd like to shag you then even though he's never overstepped the line?"

"My arrogant male ego I expect, I reckon everyone fancies me." He laughed. "I'm sure I'm wrong about that, it's my imagination that's all. I'm positive."

Slapping her arse he grabbed a cup and took it into the bedroom.

"I'd ask you to join me in the shower but I don't think I'd ever get to work."

"Sounds good to me," she called after him laughing.

She wandered around the flat touching the exquisite furnishings and state-of-the-art media equipment. To have this place to themselves even for a few weeks was wonderful and she felt elated. It was like a dream, just like her favorite film 'Pretty Woman' she thought grinning. She'd landed this amazing man, was having his baby and was living in a million pound apartment in London, then she remembered her parents reaction and her mood instantly crashed. She hadn't heard from them since she'd told them about Tom and the baby and didn't want to contact them for fear that they would still be angry.

* * *

The blue jelly felt cold on her stomach and as the ultrasound wand floated over her full bladder she squirmed. "Try and keep still and we'll try and get a proper look for you." The radiographer was very kind and smiled at her warmly.

Tom squeezed her hand.

The screen lit up and they both stared at the monochrome image. Completely transfixed. "That's the heart, beating away nicely, two arms, two legs, see the little fingers and toes." She pointed to the screen.

"Oh my God, I can't believe it, that's amazing. It's a real little person, look at it, Luce just look."

Without moving her eyes from the screen she nodded, too overcome to speak. Only now could she begin to acknowledge how scared she'd been for her baby. How convinced she'd been that her baby would be doomed like Kirsty's.

Relief washed over her and warm tears ran down her face and onto his hand as she brought it to her lips, and kissed it.

"Would you like to know the sex?" Their eyes met and grinning, both answered together.

"Yes."

"Ok then, let's see what we've got."

Endless seconds passed and eventually the radiographer stopped the cursor over the baby's groin. "It's a boy, congratulations." Both peered at the tiny penis and grinning childishly they kissed.

* * *

Pulling up outside Lucy's house Tom's hands were shaking. "Are you sure this is a good idea?"

"Yes, of course, they've got to meet you sooner or later and now we've got a copy of the scan pictures for them it will help. They'll be so distracted by their grandson they won't care if I've been knocked up by Shrek."

"Cheers, Luce that helps. NOT."

She turned to him and took his face in her hands. "Trust me, it'll be horrible but the longer we put this off the worse it'll be. We have to do this."

"I know. Come on then."

He followed her towards the door and before they could knock the door opened.

"I saw you sat outside, come in." Her mother's face was pale and drawn.

"Mum this is Tom." He extended his hand and tried to smile.

"Mrs Millson, pleased to meet you." She looked at his hand and turned away.

Lucy reached for it instead and held it tight, smiling reassuringly.

Her father was sitting in the lounge staring at the news.

"Dad, this is Tom." Slowly he turned his head and stared at Tom, standing he was at least four inches shorter than Tom but the waves of anger and intimidation rolling off him made him seem so much more frightening than the dad she knew and loved.

Getting up from his chair he glared at both of them.

"I love my daughter and I want her to be happy. I'm furious she's with someone old enough to be her father and I hear you're married, that makes you a total bastard in my book and you'll no doubt cheat on Lucy one day too. But she's made her bed and this baby is our grandchild so we'll stand by her but you...you've got a long way to go before I change my opinion about you. You'd better be a better partner to her than you were to your wife or I will fucking kill you, do you hear me?" His finger was inched from Tom's face but he didn't waver.

"Mr Millson, I appreciate your honesty and I don't blame you, but believe me I will do everything in my power to look after Lucy and our son. I promise."

"Son?"

"Yes dad we have the scan pictures, here." She thrust them into her father's hand and as he stared at the small prints his face broke into a huge smile.

"Lucy they're beautiful."

Seizing her chance she sat down next to her father and put her arm round his shoulders. She quickly glanced over her shoulder at Tom and winked.

"KAREN, KAREN," he called. "Come and see these they're amazing, it's a boy."

Tentatively Lucy's mother entered the room.

"Stop shouting. I'm here. Let me see then." He handed them over and Lucy saw her mother's eyes fill with tears.

"Oh he's gorgeous, really beautiful, Luce. You must be so relieved?"

"Yes, we both are aren't we, Tom?"

She gestured towards him to include him in the group.

"Do you have any other children, by your wife or any other girlfriends, Tom?"

Her mother asked almost casually, still staring at the scan pictures. He felt himself bristle but refused to rise to the bait.

"No. Just this one with Lucy."

"Well at least none you know about eh? Time will tell I suppose."

"Despite what you think I don't make a habit of cheating or getting women pregnant."

"Really? Just our twenty-two year old daughter then. Lucky Lucy."

"MUM! Stop it will you, Tom's a part of this family now and if you want to see this baby grow up you better accept him." Moving to stand beside him she clutched his hand, "we love each other."

Slowly turning to look Tom in the eye her mother challenged him. "Is that right, Tom? Do you love Lucy?"

"Of course. What's not to love? She's beautiful, amazing, loving, fun, intelligent, how could I not love her, I'm lucky to have found her."

"That's not what I asked you. Do you love her?"

"Mum leave him alone. He's answered you."

Tom blushed deeply as Karen stared at him.

"Tom, come into the kitchen and help me with the tea please."

He looked into Lucy's eyes and she nodded. Entering the kitchen-diner he hovered awkwardly in the doorway, unsure what to do.

"Please, take a seat, Tom."

"Thanks." He toyed with the idea of sitting as far away from Karen as possible but decided to appear confident and sat near where she stood by the kettle. Without looking at him she said, "Tom, for what it's worth, thanks for standing by Lucy and supporting her with the baby."

"Erm...that's ok. What else would I do?"

"Some men your age who had gotten a young woman pregnant wouldn't have done that, at least you're doing the right thing. I know you don't love her although the way you answer her it probably gives the impression you do without actually lying. That's kind."

"She deserves better than me, I know that, I'm sorry she got pregnant, it wasn't meant to happen but it did and I won't let her down. I adore her, she's amazing and I completely understand why you're angry. I would be too."

"Her dad's all piss and wind, he wouldn't hurt a fly really but he's right though, you have to promise not to hurt her."

"I will do everything I can to make her happy."

"What about your wife?"

Karen sat down next to him as the tea brewed.

"Things had been bad for months, I wasn't looking for an affair, Lucy and I became friends and it just happened. I've told Sophie, she knows everything."

"That was brave and quite honorable I suppose."

"Not really, you give me far too much credit, I knew how much it would hurt her and I just didn't want her hearing it through the grapevine."

"For what it's worth I get the impression Lucy could have done a lot worse than you."

She smiled.

"Thank you for that."

"Don't let me down."

"I won't." He allowed himself a smile as relief washed over him.

"Would you carry the tray for me please?" Without waiting for his reply she walked ahead of him into the lounge.

Lucy and her father sat side by side on the sofa; they appeared to be chatting casually. As Tom entered the conversation stopped and her father glared.

"Dad, please," Lucy implored but it was her mother who spoke.

"It's ok, Jack. I've spoken to Tom and we've sorted a few things out, I think we should make an effort. He's family now."

For several moments their eyes met and something unspoken passed between them. Silently Jack nodded just once.

CHAPTER 15

Alex reached over to caress Kirsty's breast. They always slept naked and he often cuddled up to her and fell asleep holding her breast so she didn't immediately respond.

"Sweetheart," he breathed into her neck.

"What?"

He responded by pressing his erection into her buttocks and running his hand down her stomach towards her pubic hair.

"Let's make love. It's time to get back to normal. I want you." She rolled over and in the darkness they kissed.

"You should be ovulating now so it's the ideal time."

Silently she took him in her hand and began to run her palm up and down his shaft.

"Ooh that's gorgeous." In response he ran a finger down between her thighs and began to worm it inbetween her outer lips, burrowing, searching for her clitoris.

They continued to stimulate each other for some time and as he felt her body gradually respond and the moisture on his hand he eased her legs apart. "You're so gorgeous, I love you so much."

"I love you too."

Wordlessly they maneuvered into their favorite position and with his body nestled behind her he gently entered her. They both gasped as he held still for several minutes. Slipping her leg over his, she allowed her thighs to open wide and reaching for her clitoris with his hand he rubbed her small fold as it grew under his touch. As she began to give herself over to the sensation he started to move within her wet folds in rhythm with his hand and as she came he let himself climax inside her. Without moving he soon fell asleep. With their bodies still spooned together as his cock withered and their combined juices soaked into the sheet, she lay, staring, wide-eyed, into the darkened room.

* * *

"TOM! TOM!! Shit...TOM HELP ME!"

He was shaken awake by the shouting coming from the bathroom. It was two twenty-seven am. "What's the matter. Is there a spider in the bath?"

As he walked through the door he took in her white face and the blood on her hands and down her legs.

"Fuck." He took her in his arms and guided her into the shower. "Rinse it off sweetheart; I'll get your clothes."

"What do I do?" She whimpered helplessly.

"Let's go to the hospital. I'll get dressed."

As she reached for the showerhead she was gripped by a ferocious, cramping pain and she doubled over. "Ahhh!"

"Lucy, look at me."

"It hurts...it hurts."

"I know babe."

Carefully he rinsed her legs and hands and dressed her as she doubled over in pain. "Where are your pads Luce?...Look at me, you need a pad, for the blood."

"I don't have any, I don't need them."

"Oh shit of course. Here let me put this in your pants." Rolling up several hand-full's of toilet paper he placed them in her pants and redressed her. She was bleeding heavily. Taking a hand

towel for the car he helped her into the passenger seat but no sooner had he pulled away
than she was screaming. The ten minute drive
was interminable and as Tom screeched to a
halt outside A&E he dragged her from the car
and carried her into the department. The towel
and her clothes were soaked and she was silent
in his arms, eyes closed. "Luce, we're here it's
ok now."

She didn't respond. "LUCE...LUCE!! HELP
SOMEONE PLEASE. SHE'S BLEEDING."

Staggering into the reception area several
staff ran towards them and placed Lucy onto a
trolley and before he'd had time to register she
had been whisked away behind swing doors.

His clothes were soaked with blood.

"Hello, sir can you give me some of your
daughter's details."

"She's not my daughter, she's my partner,"
he growled.

"Oh gosh, I'm so sorry sir, can I have her details please, full name, date of birth, address,
GP's address."

He stared at the tactless receptionist and realized he didn't know if Lucy had a middle name,
her date of birth or her GP and he only knew the
road she lived in, he hadn't noticed the number.

"I'm afraid I don't know all the stuff you need."

"Just give me what you know then, I'll find
her on the system. Has she been a patient here
before?"

"I don't know. It's Lucy Millson; she's twenty-
two and lives in Summerton road, Norden."

After several moments staring at the computer
she smiled. "I have her, I'll buzz you through,
take a seat and someone will call for you when
she's been seen ok?"

In a daze he walked through the swing doors, down the corridor to the waiting area and sat down. Too numb to cry he kept seeing the blood and her face so pale and scared, and the pain. She'd been in agony. He just wanted to see her. Standing up he approached the nurse's station. The department was relatively quiet, and he thanked God it was a weekday. The nurse at the desk smiled kindly.

"Lucy Millson, I'm her partner, can I see her please?"

"I'm sorry the doctors are working on her at the moment, she's lost a lot of blood, take a seat and I'll see what's happening for you."

"NO!! I WON'T TAKE A SEAT," "JUST LET ME SEE HER."

The nurse stood up and moved away from him, and suddenly two security officers were flanking him and had his arms in a firm grip.

"Nice and quietly now sir sit yourself down." They walked him to his seat and sat either side of him.

"I just want to see her that's all," he growled.

As Tom sat with his head in his hands the nurse disappeared. After sometime she returned and crouching down in front of him she placed a cool hand on his shoulder.

"Mr Millson, you can come through now."

Without correcting her he mutely followed through the swing doors into the centre of the department.

She drew back the curtain and as he looked into the cubicle he saw Lucy on a trolley, dressed in a hospital gown that looked far too big for her, connected to a blood transfusion, an oxygen monitor and a blood pressure machine.

As she saw him she burst into tears.

He tentatively reached for her trying to avoid the equipment but she ignored the apparatus and fell into his arms sobbing and at last he started to cry.

"He's dead, Tom. We lost our baby."

"I know hun, I know." He stroked her hair and thought about the scan pictures and how happy they'd been just a few days before.

"Mr. Millson."

A young, clearly exhausted doctor stood at the end of the trolley. "We have to take your wife to theatre I'm afraid. We need to be sure that she doesn't retain what we call products of conception that could cause an infection. The procedure is performed under light general anesthetic and she'll be home tomorrow. You can start trying again next month and this shouldn't affect your ability to have more children, unfortunately, spontaneous miscarriage happens to lots of women."

"So…the baby?"

"I'm sorry."

As they wheeled the trolley away to theatre he held Lucy's hand until the last minute.

* * *

The car was a mess, the seat soaked with Lucy's blood. He rubbed his hand over his face and sighed. It was four fifteen. He considered dropping the car off at the valeters, leaving them a voicemail and getting a taxi to the flat but decided against it.

The lights were all blazing when he entered the apartment and there was blood in the bathroom and all over the bed. He worked methodically through the bedroom, stripping the sheets and binning them along with the towels. Then he scrubbed. The wet-room tiles and floor cleaned up well but the bedroom carpet seemed unsalvageable, the more he rubbed the worse it looked. The mattress would have to go too.

Sitting back on his knees he noticed it was light. It was seven thirty. He was exhausted. He couldn't face work.

The dealership's out of hours answer machine kicked in. "Hi it's Tom Wilkes, I won't be in to-day, I've been at the hospital all night with a friend, I'll phone later about tomorrow, cheers."

Unable to face the decimated bedroom he lay down on the sofa and slept.

CHAPTER 16

Opening his eyes slowly Tom became aware of the phone ringing. "Hello?"

"Mr Millson? It's staff nurse on the gynae ward at St Georges." Springing to his feet he became immediately alert. "What's happened, is she ok?"

"Lucy's fine, I'm just ringing to say she's back from theatre and she'll be ready to go home in about an hour, she'll need some clothes to go home in too please."

"Oh ok, no worries, thanks."

Ending the call Tom began to relive the previous night, as he wandered into the bedroom he took in the stained carpet and ruined mattress and knew he couldn't bring Lucy back to the flat.

Pausing to consider his options he glanced at the clock and noticed he'd only slept for about three hours.

"Shit," he muttered as he rubbed his hands over his face. Feeling the stubble and noticing how stained his clothes were he headed for the shower but as he stepped into the wet-room he only saw Lucy's face, white and scared and the blood.

Opting to use Andy's shower he washed, shaved and changed as quickly as possible, then made some strong coffee.

Firing up his laptop he found a professional carpet cleaning company and booked an urgent appointment, followed by an order for a new super-kingsize mattress, bed linen and towels. Lastly he phoned the valeting company used by the dealership and arranged to drop the demonstrator off on the way to the hospital. He told them he'd picked up a dog that had been hit by a car and had taken it to the vets. Not terribly convincing he thought, but he was hoping to avoid awkward questions.

* * *

They'd removed the drip and cannula from her arm, she'd had a hot drink and a sandwich, she'd been out of bed and been to the loo and as far as the nursing staff and doctors were concerned she was 'fine to go home' but as she sat huddled in the bed in the theatre gown acutely aware of the huge hospital issue sanitary towel between her legs held in place by elastic net knickers she felt anything but 'fine'.

The door opened and as Tom walked in, holding an enormous bouquet of roses, she dissolved into floods of tears. "Oh sweetheart, it's ok." He took her in his arms and stroked her hair and face as he kissed her forehead.

Unable to speak he held her until the sobbing quietened and her breathing calmed.

"I'm so sorry Tom, I'm so, so, sorry."

Holding her by the shoulders he held her at arm's length and looked into her eyes. "What are you on about? You've got nothing to be sorry for, these things happen, it's not your fault, don't say things like that."

"The doctor said that but I lost our baby, he died inside me, for some reason he just died and it feels like my fault. It hurts so much."

Holding her again he resumed stroking her hair. "I know, I know, but you'll feel better soon, I promise, things will get better just give yourself some time. The nurses told me before I came in that we both have to realize your hormones are making you teary and sometimes anesthetic can make people over-emotional too, it's to be expected."

"I guess you're right."

"Crying's ok, don't hold it in. Let it out."

Attempting a weak smile she hugged him and kissed him softly on the cheek. "Let's go home."

"Ah...that might be a bit of a problem, you might want to go and stop at your mum's for a couple of days, just until the flat's sorted out."

"What? Why can't I come home with you?"

"I just have a few things to sort out first."

"Like what?"

"Lucy, just think about last night for a minute."

Her hand flew to her face and she blanched. "Oh my God, the flat, the mess, oh Tom, I'm so sorry I didn't think about you going back to that, it must have been awful for you."

Placing a finger on her lips he hushed her. "Sweetheart, whatever I did last night wasn't a tenth of what you went through so don't give it another thought."

"But Tom, the car?" Her eyes grew wide with alarm.

"At the valeters as we speak, it's all taken care of ok? Get dressed, let's get out of here."

"I can't go back to mum's, she doesn't know yet."

"What?... Oh shit. I didn't ring her and you obviously couldn't."

"She'll be so upset that she wasn't here with me."

"Lucy," he said taking her hand. "It's done now and we can't go back in time and ring her she'll just have to let it go, I'll talk to her, you get dressed."

"Are you sure?"

"Leave it with me."

* * *

"Karen. Hi, it's Tom."

"Tom? Is everything ok?"

"No I'm afraid it's not. Lucy lost the baby last night, we're at St Georges now, getting ready to leave."

"What? And you're only ringing me now?"

Her voice began to rise in anger.

"Hang on a minute, it was a real emergency, she lost a lot of blood and had to have a transfusion and go to theatre. I've been up all night trying to make the flat habitable again, as it is I've got to get a new mattress and have the carpet cleaned. Lucy was my first concern and I didn't see any point in waking you up to come down here and sit in the corridor waiting when she needs you now, she needs to come home with you until the flat is sorted."

"Yes, of course, you're right. I'm sorry Tom, how are you coping? It was your baby too, you must be feeling pretty fragile?"

"Actually, I think I'm still in shock, oh my God, there was so much blood and she looked so pale and lost. The blood was everywhere, it was awful, I can still see her in the bathroom screaming, it was dreadful. I'll never forget it. I haven't stopped to think about the baby yet, I was so worried about Luce."

He heard her choke back a sob.

"Oh shit. I'm sorry, Karen; I didn't mean to blurt it out like that."

"Thank you for taking good care of her, Tom you did everything right. I'll expect you in about an hour then, give her a kiss for me."

"Thanks for that. See you."

PART 3
SUMMER

CHAPTER 17

They lay side by side gazing up at the ceiling. It was a glorious, hot, summer Sunday morning and the room was filled with the sounds of lawnmowers and playing children.

"Let's go on holiday."

"We can't afford it."

"Please, Alex just for a week," rolling to face her he smiled.

"We are supposed to be trying for a baby, all our savings have to cover all the expenses, we don't have any spare cash babe, sorry." She turned away and rose from the bed.

"Kirst...what's the matter?"

"Nothing. It's nothing."

"It doesn't look like nothing."

"I just...no it's ok."

Getting up he walked over to her and took her in his arms. "Come back to bed, we've got something important to do," he grinned as he nudged her thighs with his rapidly hardening penis.

"I don't feel like it ok?"

"But you're supposed to be ovulating for the next couple of days so we really need to get stuck in," he laughed and took her hand. "No pun intended." She pushed him away and he landed on the bed.

"How would you know when I'm ovulating? What is it with you? They're my periods, my ovaries and my cycle, you're like a bloody stuck record."

"Kirsty, what the fuck's going on? I just keep a track of your cycle so we both know when to make love to achieve a pregnancy, that's all. Why is that a problem hun?"

"'Achieve a pregnancy'," she mimicked. "Listen to yourself would you? Why can't we just stop trying for a bit and have some fun, relax. I love you but right now you're putting so much pressure on me I'm hardly likely to change my mind at this rate."

"Change your mind about what? I thought we both wanted to try for another baby."

"Well, *we* don't, *I* don't actually." Sitting down next to him she took his face in her hands and looked into his eyes.

"I'm on the pill."

"You what?" Anger flared in his eyes and he pulled his face away. Putting her hands back she continued. "I love you so much and I want a baby, lots of babies with you, but it's too soon, I haven't gotten over it yet, I need to grieve, please try to understand. I just need a little time."

"But you lied to me."

"No, I just didn't tell you, I didn't want to hurt you. I just planned to take it for a few months then stop when I felt ready."

"So you were deceiving me then?"

"Please don't be angry."

"This really hurts."

"I know and I'm sorry, really but just be patient."

"I can't believe you went behind my back like this."

"I'm sorry I didn't tell but I'm not sorry I decided to wait, it's too soon. I'm too raw and too scared, it wouldn't be fair. Please try to understand."

"I do, but I'm so disappointed you didn't feel you could talk to me."

"Alex, sweetheart." She kissed him softly on the lips. "I couldn't talk to anybody about how

I felt, until now, that is. I want babies with you but I need to deal with the loss first, I just have to do this. Please understand."

He leaned forward and kissed her deeply.

"I do understand. I guess I can't really appreciate what you went through at the clinic. It was hard enough for me to watch you and I just thought I could blot it out by pretending it didn't happen. I never really faced up to the fact that our baby died until you just talked about grieving. I think I wanted to get pregnant to help me forget." His voice started to crack with emotion as his eyes filled with tears. "Despite everything, she was our daughter and I miss her so much, I can't believe it happened, I've tried to blot it out but it's not working." Tears ran down both their faces as she rested her head on his shoulder.

"I'm so sorry I was so insensitive, you must think I'm a total shit banging on about ovulation and pregnancy all the time, forgive me?"

"I knew it was your way of dealing with it, but I did feel like you were in charge of my ovaries and not me. Never heard of ovary envy before, what would Freud have made of that?"

Laughing he lay back on the bed and drew her on top of him.

"How about we make love,-no agenda, have brunch and then go out and buy a really pretty pink rose-bush for the garden?"

"Sweetheart, that would be perfect, thank you."

They kissed and as her nipples hardened against his chest he gripped her buttocks and pulled her into him. She knew she was already wet and as she straddled him she fingered herself to moisten her fingers and began to stroke the shaft, using her juice to lubricate her hand.

Taking her hand he sucked her fingers one by one, as he stared into her eyes. "You taste good but I need to taste you properly," he grinned. "Come up here."

She shuffled on her knees until she was kneeling over his face and as he licked and nuzzled at her he felt her warm wetness on his face. Kirsty gripped the headboard and started to move her hips in time to Alex's tongue inside her. Within moments she was coming and he felt her opening pulsating and gripping his tongue as he pushed further inside her. She was soaked and he loved the taste of her.

As her orgasm subsided she moved herself back down his body to his hips and as she lowered herself onto his waiting cock she started to come again. He pushed into her whilst letting her find her rhythm. She leant forward so that her clitoris was rubbing against him and he knew he couldn't hold out much longer. Within minutes they were coming together and as she lay down on top of him, exhausted and sweating she kissed each nipple, in turn before kissing his mouth.

"I love you."

"Love you more," and they both grinned.

* * *

As hard as she tried Sophie couldn't get her favorite jeans done up.

"Bollocks," she cursed as she struggled with the zip.

"Oh baby," she cooed as she stroked her swollen belly. "Looks like mama needs some new clothes."

The past four months had resulted in every check-up and appointment indicating her daughter was developing perfectly normally and that she was a fit and healthy first time mother. The scan pictures went everywhere with her and now the alleged danger period had passed she'd happily told everybody her news.

Scanning her wardrobe for leggings and a baggy shirt she dressed and after looking in the mirror she had to acknowledge she finally looked pregnant. Grinning she caressed her tiny bump and again her heart ached for Tom. She desperately longed to share this with him, to have him come to clinic with her, to have him feel the bump and notice the changes in her body. She missed his touch, his voice, his body, she longed for him as she eased her vibrator between her thighs at night and as she felt the weight of her swollen breasts in her hands in the shower. She knew it wasn't just sexual frustration, she knew she loved him and always would but she couldn't let go of the anger and resentment that he was sharing a pregnancy with someone else when she was having to cope alone. Part of her wanted to tell him just to make him pay, emotionally and financially, but she knew she would never go down that road. She resigned to cope alone.

CHAPTER 18

Karen sat down at Tom's desk, the summer sunshine was reflecting off of the huge mirrors and the highly polished cars and for a moment he was unsure whether his eyes were deceiving him. She smiled, "Hi, Tom I'm Mrs Barnes, it's my maiden name, sorry to trick you but I needed some time alone with you, hope that's ok?"

"Sure," he smiled. "Be nice to get out in the sunshine for a bit, shall we go?"

Picking up the keys he led her out to the car-park. Despite his calm exterior in front of his colleagues his mind was racing.

"This sounds important, should I be worried?"

"It is important. Can you drive somewhere quiet? A back street close by will be fine."

"Ok."

Within several minutes they were parked in a small side road, directly opposite the alley where Tom and Lucy had screwed, he smiled to himself, the irony amusing him.

Turning off the engine he opened both their windows and turned to face her.

"Ok, I'm all ears." She took a deep breath and appeared unsure whether to continue.

"Tom...I'm gonna ask you to do something for Lucy that will probably be very hard for you and will initially cause her a lot of pain and heartache."

"O...k."

"I want you to make her finish with you; I want you to start treating her really badly."

"What the hell for?"

"Because you don't need to be with her anymore, if it hadn't been for the baby you wouldn't

121

have been together. You did the right thing and I'll always appreciate that but let's face it, this relationship is purely sexual and you'll soon get bored."

"That's not fair, Lucy's lovely and I care about her."

"I know but you don't love her and you probably never will, but *she* loves *you* so she needs to finish it, to fall out of love with you, so she can move on without being too damaged by this whole debacle."

"You're asking me to break your daughter's heart then. Is that it?"

"No. Just treat her badly, be inattentive, forget to call, don't let her stay over, call her a cab instead of dropping her back, and most of all... start being a shit in bed and she'll soon want to end it with her pride intact. She'll think you're a knob and she's had a lucky escape."

Tom laughed bitterly. "You're not asking much then? Shit, I'd hate to piss you off, lady. Do you really think she deserves to be treated that badly after what she's been through? You made me promise not to hurt her and now you're asking me to do just that."

"Quite frankly, I think she deserves more than you and she deserves to be with someone who loves her, you don't, and you never will. To you girls like Lucy will always be available to be swept off their feet and shagged senseless." Her tone softened, "Tom, please, let her go."

"You are having a laugh, we're good together, she's amazing and I love being with her."

"What's her favorite color?"

"What?"

"Come on Tom, you know her so well, what's her favorite color? What was the name of her guinea-pig? Who's her best friend? What's her shoe size?"

"Do any of those things matter? Really?"

"In a committed relationship, yes. I'm just trying to point out that what you have is sexual, not substantial, did you know she wants to try for another baby ASAP?"

"Shit."

Tom looked out of the window at the alley and went through his memories of Lucy one by one. There were beautiful breasts, a wet pussy, long legs, soft lips, a great arse and then the miscarriage. There weren't any real dates, no hand-holding, no trips to the movies, no meals out, as she said, no substance, just sex.

Silently he nodded.

"You'll do it then?"

"Yes. You're right, she does deserve better." He turned to face her again. "Karen you're a great mother you know, your girls are lucky to have you."

"If I was such great mother she wouldn't have slept with a married man she hardly knew and gotten pregnant through pure carelessness. Don't flatter me, Tom this is damage limitation, I'm afraid."

"One thing."

"Yes?"

"Jack's not gonna rip my balls off when I break Lucy's heart is he?"

She smiled. "No, actually, this was his idea."

"Really?"

"He loves her so much he doesn't want her to yearn for you or idolize you, he wants her to hate your guts."

"Oh...nice, thanks Jack."

"Can't blame him."

"No I guess not."

"Shall we go back now?"

"I take it you won't be buying the car then?"

Smiling she placed her hand on his forearm, "unfortunately, no, but thanks for the ride."

* * *

His mobile rang as he opened the door to the flat, his caller ID showed it was Lucy, he rejected the call. Standing in the hallway he noticed two suitcases and called out. "HELLO?"

Andy's face appeared from his bedroom. Tom grinned back. "Hiya fuck-face, welcome back."

"Nice to see you too dick-head."

Laughing they hugged warmly.

"Fucking hell mate, I've missed your ugly face around here."

"Just checking you hadn't smashed the place up whilst I've been gone. No Lucy?"

"Er...long story actually."

"Good. I've got duty-free and I'm on New York time so tell me all." They took a bottle of Jack Daniels and two glasses onto the balcony and sat down to enjoy the evening sunshine.

Tom took the scan pictures from his wallet and handed them to Andy. "Wow, that's fantastic."

"Our son, he would have been born in October."

"'Would have been', what does that mean?"

"Lucy had a horrendous miscarriage, lost a shit-load of blood, it was awful, she had to have a transfusion and go to theatre. Tell you this place looked like the set of The Texas Chain Saw Massacre."

"Shit, that's awful. I'm so sorry. Hang on, what do you mean this place? It happened here?"

"Yeh in the middle of the night, there was blood everywhere but before you panic, I replaced

everything except the carpet which I had pro-
fessionally cleaned. It's all good I promise."

"Thanks for that but you didn't have to, and
that's not what I meant. I was just thinking
how fucking awful it must have been for both of
you, I wish you'd told me I'd have come back
sooner."

"I was fucking terrified actually."

"I bet. Thanks for putting everything right
though but is she ok? Can she still have kids?"

"Oh yeh, she's fine. It's just she won't be having them with me."

"Well you won't like it but I say thank God."

"Believe it or not her mother came into the
showroom this aft and booked a test-drive under her maiden name so she could talk to me in
private to ask me to start treating Luce like shit
so that she chucks *me.*"

Andy laughed, "you've got to admit it's a good
idea and shouldn't be too hard to do, after all
you had no plans to stay with her until she told
you she was pregnant."

"True but I left Soph partly because I couldn't
stop thinking about fucking her."

"What's wrong with that? Doesn't mean you
have to spend the rest of your life with her,
nothing wrong with a little fantasy."

"I must tell you, she had a weird theory about
why you hated her."

"Oh yeh...go on." Andy responded without
meeting Tom's gaze.

"She said you were jealous."

"Of what?"

"Of her, that you were in love with me. I told
her that was shite 'cause you wouldn't have gotten on with Sophie so well would you if you had
a thing for me. I'm right aren't I?"

Andy laughed.

"The reason I took exception to her,-I never hated her, was simply that I could see you were getting shafted, it's that simple mate, really. You know I love you as a brother but you're really not my type. I'm flattered though."

"Cheers mate. What's wrong with me then?"

"Shut up twat." They both grinned as they re-filled their glasses.

Andy sneaked a sideways glance at Tom. "Seriously, seeing me with Mike, it didn't turn you on, even a little bit?"

Tom swung round to face his companion laughing. "A ha! I bloody knew it, you do have a thing for me...after all these years. You twisted fuck."

Andy grinned sheepishly and blushed. "Worth a try eh? You're fit that's all, I certainly wouldn't kick you outta bed."

"I'll take that as a compliment, if I ever fancy going brown town I'll let you know."

"I've waited this long I can wait as long as it takes."

"You've got a fucking long wait mate, I'm telling you."

"No worries."

Tom's mobile rang again.

"Yeh." After a few seconds he replied. "No sorry I can't Andy's back and we're going up west, got some VIP tickets for some private strip club, tell you what though, when I get back I'll text you and you can get a cab over and we can meet up for a fuck."

Both men grimaced.

"Don't be so arsy, Luce." Andy could hear her raised voice.

"Look I'll text you when I can alright. I think I'm gonna be busy for a bit ok?"

Frowning Tom feigned disinterest. "Suit your-self. See ya."

Andy stared at Tom. "Ouch, don't know who that hurt more, you or her. Poor cow."

"Shut up. I feel like a complete bastard as it is."

Refilling his glass Andy reached over and squeezed his shoulder. "For what it's worth you're doing the right thing. Really."

"Why does doing the right thing feel like shit? She was really upset, and I bet you if I text her at four am she'd still turn up in her sexiest un-derwear, wet and raring to go."

"Probably," Andy agreed, nodding.

"Did you fancy going up west tonight? I could do with some serious distraction?"

"Don't mind, yeh why not?"

"Getting completely trollied, a trip to the club?"

"Sounds like a plan." They both stood and made their way inside, clutching their empty glasses.

"One for the road, well the bedroom actually my good man." Tom held his glass out.

"Excellent plan I think," Andy replied gestur-ing towards the half empty whisky bottle.

Both glasses were refilled and as Tom disap-peared into his room Andy called out, "I better check your outfit before we leave; you straight guys can't dress to save your lives."

Tom responded by running out of his room and into Andy's brandishing a hand towel and flicked him on his buttocks just as his jeans dropped to the floor.

"OY...YOU DICK HEAD! That fucking stings... I'll get you back," he shouted, rubbing his arse cheeks and grinning as Tom disappeared through the doorway.

CHAPTER 19

Lucy held the disconnected mobile in her hand and stared at the screen, her eyes were filled with tears and her hand was shaking.

Tom had completely humiliated her in front of that arsehole Andy. Trying to calm her breathing she sat down on the edge of the bed. She had hoped that Tom's feelings for her were genuine but he'd been so cold and so distant she began to think that since she'd lost the baby she'd lost him too. She was desperate to get pregnant again but he was being so fastidious about using a condom he obviously didn't want to have another baby with her. A thought entered her mind and she considered texting him to say that she'd willingly meet him at the flat for sex after his night out; she figured that if he was that pissed he might be encouraged to forget the condom.

Rifling through her underwear she brought out her sexiest outfit, all purple satin and black lace, it looked stunning with her new spray tan and blonde hair. She gazed at her breasts sadly. They'd shrunk back to her pre-pregnancy size and she knew Tom had noticed but had never said anything, in fact, he'd told her how beautiful she was. He'd been so sweet since the miscarriage and now this hateful brush-off. She realized it must be Andy's influence and, determined to win him back she picked up her phone.

* * *

As Andy and Tom sat in the back of a black cab speeding through the darkening streets of London heading west, Tom's mobile chirped.

"You're not gonna believe this." Tom was staring at his phone incredulously.

"What?"

"She's up for it, a booty call whenever we get in, look at this." He proffered his phone to Andy who gazed at the MMS picture appreciatively.

"Fucking hell, she really has the hots for you... shit."

The small screen showed Lucy dressed in seductive underwear lying on a bed with her legs open facing the camera. She'd pulled the lace of the thong to one side and was clearly pleasuring herself.

"Bollocks...now what do I do?"

"Did you really think she'd be that easy to shake off? It's gonna take quite a bit of shitty behavior before she wants rid, she's desperate, she can sense you pulling away and she's just using the one thing she knows you want. Gotta hand it to her though, she's gorgeous and she's really upped her game."

"Well, I'm gonna ignore her, but I think I might text her when we get home."

"What the fuck for? You're joking right?"

"No, I'm gonna tell her that you and me want a threesome with her, spit roast, DP the lot, that'll put her off."

"Cheers mate." Andy punched Tom's arm playfully.

"I didn't mean it like that. I meant she wouldn't do it anyway and she hates you so it's a definite no-no. Should work."

They paid the driver and headed for Andy's favorite private club. The doorman nodded as they entered. It was up a steep flight of stairs over a sex shop, the music grew louder and the staircase grew darker as they entered the bar area. The lighting was seductive and discrete. Andy gestured to the barman who quickly came over. Reaching over the bar to kiss Andy passionately the barman smiled. "Hi gorgeous, long time no see."

"Hi handsome, been in New York for a bit, did you miss me?"

"Of course. The usual?"

"Please."

Two Jack Daniels over ice arrived and as they gazed around the room they saw a table and headed to the corner. There were women and men, scantily clad and naked, dancing alone and together in various parts of the room. A voluptuous redhead caught Tom's eye and as she moved towards him he felt himself harden. She wore only a tiny, jade green thong and frighteningly high stilettos. She had huge breasts which amazingly always appeared to be natural.

She took his hand and led him through a doorway at the back of the room and into a narrow corridor. Various doors led off the passageway. She opened one and led him in. He sat in the huge leather recliner while she started some music. Sensuously she began to move to the beat and as she came closer she rubbed her breasts against his chest, turning away from him she leant over to show her bare buttocks as he playfully slapped her. Turning back to face him she took her breasts in her hands and rubbed her firm nipples whilst grinding her hips. Reaching forward he slipped a £50 note into the glass on the side-table and she smiled and began to slide the thong down her legs to the floor.

Climbing onto his lap she placed his hands on her breasts and put her head back as he tweaked each pert nipple and as he took each one in his mouth in turn she began to move her hips against his swollen crotch.

Reaching for another £50 to put in the glass she acknowledged the cash and moved to undo his flies. He was unbearably hard. She stood him to slide his trousers and pants to the floor and sitting him back in the chair she climbed onto his lap facing him again but with her arms supporting her from behind whilst her legs were spread open in front of him. He reached out to stroke her neatly waxed pussy and was mesmerized by the jewel glinting from her pierced clitoris; it exactly matched the color of her thong and stilettos. She was beautifully hot and wet and as she started to move her hips in rhythm to the music he slid two fingers into her.

She took his cock in her hand and as they stimulated each other he felt himself coming.

As his orgasm abated he opened his eyes as she wiped him off with a tissue. "Mmm, Amber that was fantastic...you're gorgeous."

She grinned, "Thanks, glad you enjoyed it, I have more time if you want to stay and play a bit longer."

"Ooh that's tempting," as she stroked his semi-flaccid cock he felt it coming back to life.

He leant forward and kissed each nipple in return, he knew better than to attempt to kiss her on the mouth.

Afterwards, when she'd helped him clean up and he'd put an extra £50 in the glass he made his way back to the bar to wait for Andy. He watched as Amber made her way over to another punter and smiled.

Andy appeared after about twenty minutes grinning. "Money well spent mate?"

He asked taking his place next to Tom. "Hell yeh. Amber, she's amazing."

"I myself had the lovely Mimi."

"Ooh you kinky bastard. Any good?"

"I'll show you the bruises later, she's so twisted, and I love it."

"You're a freak do you know that?"

Slapping Tom on the arm he replied, grinning, "abso-fucking-lutely. Drink?"

* * *

Her mobile chirped and as she grabbed the phone she noticed the message was from Tom. It was four thirteen am.

Shakily, her breath coming in gasps, she read the text.

'Hi just got in bit pissed but up 4 a bit of fun Andy liked the foto + thought u mite like a 3way maybe spit roast or dp you name it wot do u think. tb'

Her face flushed and her hand shook. He'd shown Andy that photo, that intimate photo of her bits that had been meant for his eyes only. Ripping the purple satin and lace from her body she threw it in the corner and fell on the bed sobbing.

CHAPTER 20

Karen looked at Lucy's bloodshot swollen eyes and felt her heart break. She'd heard her daughter crying on and off all night. Lucy sat down at the table still in her dressing gown and rested her head in her hands. She looked exhausted.

"Tea?"

"Please."

"Any toast love?"

"No ta."

She brought the mug to the table and sat down next to Lucy and took her hand.

"What's wrong love?"

"Nothing mum, I'm fine." Looking up she forced a smile.

"Is everything ok with you and Tom?"

Breaking down Lucy fell into her mother's arms. Between sobs she explained about how cold Tom had been towards her and the fact that he'd chosen to spend time with Andy rather than with her.

Karen nodded sympathetically.

"Sweetheart, Andy's just got back from America, they've got a lot of catching up to do, it's natural for them to want to go out together."

"Mum it wasn't just that." Lucy started to shake her head. "He did something that's unforgivable, I sent him a very personal text and he showed it to Andy and then he suggested I do something vile, with both of them, it was horrible."

"Are you sure? Didn't you say they were drunk and that they'd been in Soho watching strippers or something. That sounds like drink talking if you ask me, invite him for lunch today, I bet he turns up with a huge bunch of flowers and an even bigger apology."

"Do you really think so?"

There was so much hope in her daughter's eyes that it took all Karen's strength to sit there and lie to her.

As Lucy reached for her phone Karen stopped her, "tell you what, get dressed, get a cab and surprise him."

"Shall I?"

"I would."

Lucy grinned.

"Thanks mum." She leant over and hugged Karen before running upstairs.

She picked up her own mobile and began to write a text.

* * *

Tom picked up the phone and read the message.

"Shit."

He started to tidy the bed and pick up his clothes then stopped.

Walking into Andy's room he shook his friend's shoulder, "fuck off."

"Got any bras mate? Oh and a couple of condoms?"

Andy sat up. "What the fuck are you on about?"

"Lucy's on her way over, I need to make it look like I shagged someone else."

"You did."

"Well yeh, almost...but not here," he grinned sheepishly.

"Oh right I get it...top drawer there's a bra someone left behind I think and Johnnys are here." He gestured towards the ornate dish on the bedside cabinet.

He handed Tom several condoms and he took them and the bra into his room.

He stuffed the bra under his pillow and put liquid soap into three condoms, tied them up and put one down the toilet without flushing, one on the bathroom floor and one hidden in the bed.

* * *

Wearing a pretty, pink summer dress over skimpy, white undies Lucy slipped from the cab and into the apartment block. Riding the lift to the penthouse she felt the familiar excitement at the thought of seeing Tom and the possibility of making love. She was already tingling with anticipation. She was determined to forgive him the stupid text. He'd been pissed and if you truly love someone you always forgive them.

She rang the bell and after a few moments Andy opened the door. He was naked and Lucy gasped in surprise.

"Well if it ain't juicy Lucy, morning, Luce how are you?"

"Is Tom here please?" Her voice trembled, but Andy had already disappeared into his room.

She opened the door slowly and looked at the disheveled bed. He was laying in the middle spread-eagled and clearly asleep. She smiled as she slipped off the dress and climbed in under the covers.

Taking his penis in her hand she started to caress the shaft tenderly. He moaned appreciatively.

Rolling to look at her his eyes widened in surprise. "Luce, what a nice surprise, I wasn't expecting you."

"Who were you expecting?" She withdrew her hand, frowning. ≈

Taking her hand he placed it back on his erection and smiled. "Only you babe, only you. Come here."

She rolled on top of him and as she spread her legs to straddle him he undid her bra and began nuzzling her breasts.

Wriggling to get out from beneath her he tried to flip her over. "Get off a minute and lay face down will you?"

"Ok."

He took her hips and pulled her bottom up so that her knees bent under her and supported her.

"Let's get these fucking things off." He ripped the lace from between her legs so ferociously that she yelped.

"Ow that hurt; oh my God did you just rip my knickers?"

"Shush now. Just relax."

Placing his hand between her thighs at the front he eased his fingers between her lips and began to tease her clitoris. He wanted her wet enough and aroused enough that she wouldn't immediately fight him off.

As she pushed her buttocks further into the air she began to rock her hips. Reaching with the other hand for a condom he rubbed her arse with lube and ripped the packet with his teeth.

As she started to climax Tom pushed his cock hard into her arse. Lucy instantly jumped. "Tom, ow, that hurts? Get off, please. Tom, STOP!"

"Keep still babe, you just need to relax, trust me."

"What the hell's going on? You know I don't like this."

"Relax it's only a little game. Calm down and you'll enjoy it I promise."

Placing his hand on the back of her neck to ensure she couldn't look round he continued to thrust into her.

"You're hurting me, Tom get off," she sobbed.

"Shut up bitch." He slapped her hard across the buttocks.

"Ow, get off me, get off me please, you're scaring me."

"Grow up, Lucy."

Forcing her head down Tom continued to drive into her until he came.

"Oh, Amber that feels so good, you're so hot and tight."

As he withdrew he heard a sob. She crawled off the bed and sat on the floor, pale and shocked.

"Who the fuck is Amber?"

"What? Amber, did I say that? It's just a joke, Lucy, come on, it's just a bit of fun. A bit of role-play that's all."

"You bastard, you absolute bastard."

"Easy. That's a bit harsh."

"Get away from me."

She crawled into the bathroom and as she approached the toilet he heard her gasp.

He leapt from the bed and threw back the quilt to reveal the used condom and quickly dragging the bra from under the pillow he laid it on top.

Sobbing she ran from the bathroom into the bedroom and as she saw the condom and bra she collapsed onto the floor crying inconsolably.

"Hey, hey sweetheart, it's ok." He put his arm around her and held her as she cried.

"Tom, I don't know you anymore what's happened to you, to us?"

"Nothing's happened to me; I just wanted to play a bit of a game that's all."

"What about the used condoms and the bra?"

"You're overreacting. I guess Andy used this room last night."

"Why?"

"Said the view was better from here that's all. I crawled in here when his date left and he went back to his own bed."

"Isn't that a bit weird?"

"We are talking about Andy." She laughed and started to relax.

"That's better; anyone would think you didn't trust me."

"Apart from the sex I came over to ask you to lunch at ours today, about one thirty?"

"That'll be really nice, thank your mum for asking me. Shall I call you a taxi?"

"What?"

He stood up, pulled her to her feet and handed her a £20 note, her dress and bra.

"A taxi, to get you home?"

"Aren't you taking me? Tom I can't go in a taxi with no knickers on."

"Course you can, I can't take you I'm still pissed. I'll see you at yours at one thirty."

Pushing her towards the door he pecked her on the cheek and pushed her out onto the landing.

"See you later."

"Tom, TOM," but the door was closed.

Sinking to the floor he hung his head in his hands and felt the tears threatening to fall.

Andy came and sat by him. "You ok?"

"NO, she doesn't deserve this."

"You're doing the right thing, seriously mate."

CHAPTER 21

Jack glanced at the clock for the fourth time. It was two ten.

"You did tell him one thirty didn't you?"

"Of course I did." Lucy glanced anxiously at her mother.

"Well I'm not waiting any longer, your mother's cooked a lovely meal and I won't see it spoiled. Karen let's dish up."

Lucy grabbed her mobile and stood.

"Please dad just a few more minutes." She began to walk towards the door, checking her phone for a message. "I'll text him, he might have been in an accident."

Her father stood up. "He'll wish he'd been in a bloody accident if I get hold of him."

Karen placed her hand on her husband's arm. "Gently, Jack."

He nodded silently as they began to serve lunch.

At the front door she scanned the road for his car. Her mobile showed no unread messages or missed calls. She dialed his mobile and it went straight to voicemail.

"Tom, where are you sweetheart? Call me please."

She stayed in the doorway hoping, willing her phone to beep. After a few minutes she reluctantly went in and closed the door behind her. Forcing a smile she entered the dining room.

"Oh what a relief. He's fine, just caught in traffic. There's been an accident." Sitting down she began to eat.

Her parents exchanged glances and noted her flushed face and reluctance to make eye contact.

"Does that mean he's on his way then?"

"Oh...erm...well, I said not to bother now. It's a bit late really isn't it?"

"Really? I thought you said he was on his way, seems silly to turn back now."

Her parents exchanged looks, aware that they were pushing Lucy too hard.

"I'll do him a plate and put it in the microwave. Once they get the road open he'll be here in no time. Whereabouts was the accident?"

Karen began loading a plate as Lucy suddenly stood up and slammed her hand on the table.

"MUM...mum, please just leave it. He's not coming ok, there is no accident. He just hasn't turned up."

Jack stood to meet his daughter's eye. "What do you mean, 'just hasn't turned up'? You mean he's stood you up, well, all of us actually?"

"Yes dad that's exactly what I mean. He's being a complete bastard, and I don't know what to do to make things the way they were."

Sobbing, she sat back down; her mother sat beside her and put a comforting arm around her.

"Maybe you can't make things the way they were?"

Pulling away Lucy glared at her mother. "DON'T YOU SAY THAT. DON'T YOU EVER SAY THAT. HE LOVES ME."

Placing a hand over Lucy's her mother said softly, "does he though? Really? Think about what he's actually said to you, has he ever said 'I love you'?"

"He's said it loads of times actually. Yes loads," she lied. "Anyway words don't mean anything, he treated me as if he loved me. He looked after me."

"Could that be because you were pregnant?"

"What's that supposed to mean?"

"When I asked him if he loved you he said you were lovable and that he cared, that's not the same thing. He wanted the baby and was prepared to stand by you, now it's just the two of you, well. Things have changed."

Jack sat down opposite the two women and reached across the table to take Lucy's other hand in his.

"Mum's right you know, he's a total bastard, a cheat and a player. He's probably already cheated on you." Lucy's eyes rose to meet her father's and with startling clarity she recalled the disheveled bed the condoms and the bra and knew her parents were right.

"But I love him, I really love him. How could this have happened?"

"Sweetheart, it was plain old-fashioned lust. You're not the first young woman to fall for the charms of an older man and you won't be the last. I know you love him but I don't believe it would have worked. Ever."

"Oh dad, I feel so stupid. He used me didn't he?"

Walking round to her side of the table he stood behind her and placed his hands on her shoulders.

"Oh love, don't blame yourself, he knew exactly what he was doing, he chose this. He could have said no, he could have chosen to stay faithful to his wife but he didn't, and if he cheated on her after ten years you can bet your bottom dollar he'll cheat on you after four months."

As her voice broke with emotion she whispered, "I think he already has."

* * *

His mobile chirped. It was Karen.
'Thank you.'
He deleted the text.

CHAPTER 22

Sophie looked at the list she'd made and the total at the bottom of the page.

"Shit."

Standing up to walk around she absently rubbed her swollen belly.

"Oh baby, we're in big trouble."

Returning to her seat she rubbed her face with her hands. She knew without doubt that there was no way she could afford even half of the essentials the baby would need. Her credit cards were maxed out and she had no spare cash at the end of each month. She couldn't afford a loan and although her parents were buying the cot they weren't in a position to lend her any money. She let her mind drift to the possibilities of second-hand shops and eBay and she felt the tears that threatened to fall. At that moment her bump fluttered and she jumped, soothing the wriggling baby with her hand she murmured, "it's ok, mama will sort it out. Don't worry little one, we'll be ok I promise." The baby continued to move for a few more minutes and she got up to walk round the room in an effort to soothe it.

Eventually the bump settled and Sophie sat back down and began to log on to eBay, and as she browsed she started to consider any items around the house that she could sell. Picking up her pen again she started a new list and when she'd finished she compared the totals from both lists. It was close enough. Feeling the tension ebb away she began walking from room to room gathering various items to photograph.

PART 4
AUTUMN

CHAPTER 23

As he pulled into the filling-station he instantly recognized her car parked on the far-side of the forecourt. He knew it was hers because of the small dent in the driver's door from when he'd parked too close to a bollard. Remembering how she'd instantly forgiven him and kissed him as he'd apologized made him smile. Scanning the garage shop he spotted her head above the display of charcoal and cheap flowers. Deciding to move his car from the pump to the parking area he ran to the shop. She was paying for some milk and as she turned their eyes met.

Starting to smile his gaze fell to her swollen stomach and suddenly rose again to her face, confused.

"Sophie...you look amazing...er...congratulations."

Walking towards him and away from the queue she smiled.

"Tom, thanks. It's good to see you. You've lost weight."

"Yeh and you seem to have gained some." He gestured towards her bump, "I didn't realize you were with someone else."

"Someone else? Why would you think that?"

"Well I'm assuming that's not wind and unless you went for a sperm donor or a one-night stand, neither of which are really your style, there was a man involved somewhere along the line. Is it twins? Sorry, but you're huge."

She smiled. "No, just one and it wasn't either of those things and I'm not with anyone else. The father doesn't know about the baby, that's all."

"You didn't tell him? That's a little harsh."

"Oh, Tom you have no idea, trust me, he really didn't deserve to know." Starting to push past him she turned.

"Surely your baby must be due in a few weeks?"

His eyes dropped to the ground and his voice sounded empty.

"We lost him, at fourteen weeks, it was a very bad miscarriage, very traumatic. We're not together anymore."

Reaching for his hand she felt her heart soften. "Oh, Tom I'm so very sorry, that's awful."

"It was pretty shit, yeh but I'm so glad you finally got what you wanted. You look fantastic, really glowing, shit...what a cliche," they both laughed.

"Thanks but believe me this little lady comes at a high price. It's hard being on your own."

"I bet...did you say 'little lady?' A girl then? That's brilliant, have you thought of a name yet?"

"I have, but it's a secret."

"Oh, ok I understand. Seriously though, you need to get the dad on board even if it's only financially. She deserves that much and you never know, he might surprise you."

"Let's see shall we?... Tom this is your baby. I was going to tell you the night you left. I'm seven months pregnant with your daughter. Surprised?" With that she pushed past him and out the door.

Tom gulped, too stunned to speak he just watched her cross the forecourt, manoeuvre her bump into her car and drive away, he couldn't see, but she was crying.

After several seconds he realized that he had to follow her.

"Fuck, fuck, fuck," he muttered as he ran to his car. Starting the engine he realized he still needed petrol. For a moment he considered chancing it but as the warning light was on he decided against it. Fumbling with the nozzle he struggled with shaking hands to fill the tank. He ran to the kiosk and cursed at the queue. Eventually he was able to run to the car and take off towards his old address.

* * *

She immediately started in the direction of home when she realized that would be the first place Tom would look for her. Cursing, she turned round and headed towards the local shopping mall. Feeling slightly out of breath she made her way to the food hall and ordered a cup of tea and as she slumped into a chair she heard her mobile ringing.

It was Tom, rejecting the call she turned the phone off and she wondered what would happen when he inevitably caught up with her.

* * *

'You have reached the voicemail service for number 0774...'

"Bollocks!!"

He hit the steering-wheel with the palm of his hand.

"Soph, ring me. Please. I'm at the house and I'll still be here when you get back. I just wanna talk."

Rubbing his hands over his face he glanced at the clock on the dashboard. He guessed she'd chosen to avoid him and had skipped off some-where. Too late for her to be at work, maybe a friend? He toyed with the idea of driving around checking out the local coffee shops but decided to stay put safe in the knowledge that presum-ably, at some point she'd have to come home.

After forty-five minutes he took the keys from the ignition and got out to take a short walk. As he pressed the remote locking fob in his hand he looked down and started to grin. In his hand, attached to the car keys, and Andy's spare keys lay the house keys.

"Excellent," he muttered as he walked to-wards the front door.

Turning the key he silently prayed that she hadn't changed the alarm code, he typed in the date of their wedding and as the beeping stopped he breathed a sigh of relief.

It felt so strange being back there after so long. Walking from room to room he stopped at the empty space on the chimney breast. So-phie's Banksy print was missing, glancing at the shelves he saw huge gaps where their CDs and DVDs used to sit. He couldn't see the wii ei-ther. The large screen TV had been replaced by the portable from their bedroom. In the dining–room the boxed canteen of cutlery they'd had as a wedding present was missing, likewise as he explored the kitchen he found the unused smoothie maker, panini press and ice-cream maker had all disappeared.

"Shit...what the fuck are you doing, Soph?"

On the stairs he was horrified to see that his framed, signed Chelsea shirt was missing.

As he ran to their bedroom he threw open the wardrobe doors. The jeans, skirts, shirts and sweaters remained but the bridesmaid dresses, few designer pieces she owned and her two designer handbags he'd bought her were gone. Her shoe rack had far more gaps than he'd remembered.

"Oh, Sophie please tell me things aren't that bad." He felt tears pricking his eyes as he thought about her struggling for money when he was living with Andy rent-free and thought nothing of paying £150 for a lap dance. This was all his fault.

Lastly he went into the small home office they'd made in the box room. Although he knew in his heart that the camera and camcorder were gone he continued to search.

* * *

She dialed the voicemail number and listened to his message. Frowning she switched her phone to silent but decided to leave it on. She'd finished her tea and was desperate for the loo. Getting to her feet from the low, plastic chair was harder than she'd thought but she eventually made her way to the Ladies. The mall was closing and the light was fading. Sophie wasn't someone who had regrets, she believed in getting things done and powering forward in life but she truly regretted giving in to Tom and telling him about the baby. A stupid, stupid, spur of the moment mistake. She knew without a doubt he would be waiting for her at home and that he would do everything he could to get back into her life. The strangest thing was that when she asked herself if that was such a bad thing she wasn't really sure of her answer. She had imagined the shock on his face, the pain and had reveled in that split second, to have the upper hand, but she hadn't thought any further than his initial reaction. She only knew that she had really missed him.

CHAPTER 24

"And'…mate. You home?"

"Hiya, yeh. In here."

Andy was stretched out on the sofa watching porn as Tom entered the flat.

The screen showed a group of men and women writhing and moaning. Tom stared absently at the mass of flesh as men penetrated women and as tongues licked various orifices. He was aware of fingers and dildos and that somewhere amongst the throng there was a black man and an Asian woman.

"Mmm…didn't we watch this one the other night?" He mused.

"No that was the original. This is the sequel. Look a lot alike though. Supposed to be hotter, harder and wetter."

"If you say so."

"Ooh nice," they said in unison as the huge black man came all over a large, blonde woman's silicone breasts.

Both laughed. Tom sat down on the sofa opposite.

"And'… have you got a minute?"

Hitting the pause button Andy sat up and looked him in the eye.

"What have you been up to dick-head? You've got that look in your eye. Last time you said that it was to tell me you'd knocked up your little bimbo?"

"See, I'd like to claim that's a bit harsh but actually you're not far from the truth."

Andy suddenly stood up, his face turning red with anger.

"YOU STUPID ARSE DON'T YOU EVER BLOODY LEARN?!"

"Whoa, whoa, how about you listen before you get on my fucking case?"

Andy perched back down on the edge of the sofa. "Go on then dick-head. Tell me the worst."

Tom took a deep breath and wandered over to the window and as he gazed out at the city lights he told Andy about meeting Sophie, the baby and his tour of the house.

Eventually he stopped and turned.

"Well?"

"Shit...I don't know what to say. Do you reckon she was telling the truth?"

"Yeh, I do."

"So what happens now?"

"I know two things for sure. First is that whether we get back together or not I want to be a part of that babies' life even if it means going to court to get access and the second is that I don't want Sophie struggling for money. I want to look on eBay and see if I can either buy back or replace all the stuff she's had to sell."

"Ok, but how you gonna do any of that if she won't speak to you or see you?"

"Well the eBay stuff is easy; I can either just store it here and take it over to her or just send it to her anonymously."

"I don't think it will take her long to realize it's from you and then she'll probably just sell it again."

"Mmm maybe you're right. I'll just buy it and eventually I'll give it all back to her."

"What was it like seeing her again? Did you feel anything?"

"She looked amazing, really glowing, that's a total cliché right but she looked so much hotter and sexier than any woman I've ever seen. I realized I'd really, really, missed her. I just wanted to kiss her and hold her and look after her, well both of them."

"Shit, even hotter than Juicy Lucy?"

"Abso-fucking-lutely."

"Now is that absence making the heart grow fonder, sexual frustration or just 'cause you have a previously undiscovered pregnancy fetish?"

"I don't think I have a thing for pregnant women although Lucy looked gorgeous with big tits, big hips and a bit of a belly on her, more to nuzzle. D'you know what I mean, more voluptuous, more womanly?"

"Oh, ok, well I definitely think you've got the horn for pregnant women, but I think there's something else going on too."

"Really?"

"Listen to yourself. You could just give her some money but no, you want to get all her stuff back, not just your stuff that's gone but all the stuff, and that says you care."

"Not really...I just...well...shit, maybe I do care. I do want her to be happy and not have to sell things that mean a lot to her. Actually I think I want to be with her."

"Mmm well that's ok but I feel she may have something to say about that. I think you're gonna have to do a bit more than buy a load of stuff off eBay to get back into her good books mate."

"I know. I've been a total wanker."

"Yep, pretty much. I agree with you mate and I like you, just imagine what she thinks?"

Both men laughed.

"Fuck off twat."

"You fuck off."

"Seriously though, where's my laptop?"

"Well actually, Tom I'm pregnant with your child and I sold it to pay for nappies and breast pads."

Tom's face broke into a huge grin as he threw a cushion at Andy's head.

"You idiot."

* * *

She couldn't see his car and the house was dark. Cautiously she slid the key into the lock and opened the door, the alarm bleeped and as she switched it off she checked to see if the system had been switched off since she'd set it. Staring at the small green screen she felt herself getting angry.

"You bastard. TOM...TOM," she called.

Silence.

Storming through the house she couldn't pinpoint anything that had been touched or moved but the alarm system told her he'd been there and that he knew how bad things had become.

Responding to her mother's agitation and the adrenaline coursing through her system the baby began to kick and wriggle.

Sophie eased herself into the armchair and began to soothe her bump.

"Sorry baby. It's ok. Don't worry."

* * *

Andy peered over Tom's shoulder as he sat at the breakfast bar staring at the laptop.

"What's her eBay seller's name?"

"Well we have a joint one so if I just..." He typed the ID and password.

"That's it, you're in. Have a look at the selling list...there's all your stuff, shit, there's loads of it."

"I know."

"Anything on buy now?"

"Yeh, pretty much all of it actually. How am I gonna do this without arousing suspicion?"

"You're gonna have to buy various bits under lots of different names but how's that gonna work with PayPal and what about a postal address. Is it even doable?"

"God knows."

"Well I could buy some stuff under some names and you could buy some and we'll do it that way but where we gonna get it posted to?"

"Bollocks."

"Can't you just tell her what you want to do?"

"No. I wanna do something special, something nice to surprise her."

"Ok, well you start setting up the accounts and I'll try and think of somewhere to send the stuff."

An hour later both had registered accounts under different names with credit card, debit card and bank details spread across the accounts. Andy had arranged for the items to be sent to various different friends' addresses across London.

Slowly they began to purchase all the items until everything was sold.

CHAPTER 25

Kirsty methodically dead-headed the pink rose-bush and as each head fell she felt the tears threaten. It was warm for late September and the bush still had many buds. Despite the tears she smiled and thought about Alex's face when she'd told him she was planning to stop taking the pill at the end of the month. He'd been over-joyed. He'd asked her if she was sure. She told him she didn't know how or why she knew it was the right time, but it just was. As she gathered the fallen dead heads and carried them to the bin she imagined herself and her children in years to come looking after the rose-bush to-gether and she became aware of the smallest flutter of excitement.

* * *

"Sophie."

"Tom."

"I thought you were never gonna take my call."

"I nearly didn't."

"We need to talk."

"I really don't think we do."

"You're joking, you tell me you're pregnant with my child and then refuse to talk to me. Even for you that's a tad unreasonable."

"Piss off, Tom."

'The other person has cleared, the other person has cleared.'

She'd hung up.

Fumbling with his phone he quickly redialed.

"Why did you hang up?"

"Because you're a total shit and I don't need you and neither does *my* baby and if you can't be civil why should I even speak to you?"

"Yeh you're right, I'm sorry. Look, Sophie this isn't about you and me this is about our daughter and her needs. I want to be a proper dad and a proper birthing partner to you; I want to go to every appointment. I'm going to be there for you, Sophie, every step of the way. I promise."

She laughed.

"News flash, you've missed the first seven months. You missed all the vomiting the fainting spells, check-ups, the ultrasound scans. You missed it all and why? Because you were with your other babies' mother and quite frankly I'm under no illusion that if you're little fuck-buddy was still knocked-up you wouldn't give a shit about us."

"That's not true and it's not fair."

"No, Tom what's not fair is you raping me, cheating and getting some tart pregnant and then thinking I'll just suck it up because your little plan B didn't pan out."

"No matter what you think of me, rest assured I think far less of myself and I am truly sorry. I have behaved like an absolute bastard and I know it. Nevertheless, Soph I'm gonna be a proper father even if I have to take you to court for access. Trust me. I'm in this for the next eighteen years and beyond."

"I'll believe it when I see it."

"Ok, let me give you some money or email me a list of stuff you need and I'll sort it."

"Yeh right."

"Try me. I mean it. Just try me."

"If I didn't know you I'd almost think you were serious."

"I am serious, I also want to know when your next appointment is and I'd like a copy of the scan pictures please."

"Really? You're gonna take time off work and come with me to have my wee tested, my belly felt and my blood pressure checked?"

"Yes."

"Ok I'll email a shopping list, the scan pictures and my next midwife appointment. If you turn up then fine, if you don't then don't you ever phone me again. I mean it."

"I'll be there."

'The other person has cleared, the other person has cleared.'

She'd already hung up.

Walking out of his bedroom and into the kitchen Tom smiled.

"Well?"

"She's gonna email me scan pictures, a list of what she needs and all her appointments."

"D'you know I reckon you could charm the knickers off a nun."

"Don't kid yourself mate she's given me a really small chance and if I cock-up that's it."

"Mmm well based on previous experience there's a fairly good chance you will cock-up and will find yourself with your cock up someone else before her waters break. You forget I know you as well as she does, if not better."

"Fuck off."

* * *

Her hands were shaking, her heart was pounding and her bump was wriggling.

Allowing herself a smile she switched on her laptop.

* * *

"What the bloody hell is this? 'Nursing bras, sanitary pads, nipple shields, nipple cream, breast pads, stretch mark cream, maternity briefs, front opening nighties'. She's having a fucking laugh, I thought I'd be shopping for baby-gros and booties."

Andy grinned. "No mate she's testing you. If you can get all that stuff then maybe she'll give you a chance. Nice one Sophie."

As he opened the first of the attachments Tom's voice dropped.

"Oh my God, look at this," he whispered.

Andy walked over to the laptop and peered over Tom's shoulder.

"Wow that's amazing, look at that, that's so beautiful."

"I know. That's my daughter, this second scan is so much more detailed than the one I have in my wallet from before 'cause it was done that much later, you can see so much." Andy squeezed his shoulder.

"That's your God-daughter."

"What...really? Erm hadn't you better ask Sophie first?"

"No, she can choose the other Godparent."

They grinned at each other.

"Time to wet the babies' head I reckon."

* * *

She felt his tongue on her nipples as his hand reached down to spread her thighs. She was wet. Gently flicking her clitoris she pushed against his hand moaning softly. She was vaguely aware that she wasn't pregnant but wasn't concerned or surprised. As he eased a finger into her she bucked and bore down on his hand desperate for him to be inside her.

"Please," she panted. "Fuck me, Tom."

Instantly her eyes flew open and she sat up.

"Tom? Where did that come from?"

She put a reassuring hand against her belly and tried to calm her breathing. The dream had been so vivid. She was tingling, wet and alive with unsatisfied sensations. Reaching over to open the drawer nearest her she pulled out her rampant rabbit. Easing it between her lips she plunged the vibrating phallus into her soaking wet opening. Within minutes she was writhing and rocking against the vibrator, her clitoris hard and engorged and her pussy throbbing and spasming as the twin heads worked her to orgasm.

As the climax abated she felt no relief, no satisfaction. She still felt hot and wet and swollen. She tried to reach down to finger herself but her bump made it impossible to get decent penetration. Using her wet fingers to massage her clitoris she began to rock again. She was incredibly horny and frustrated.

Chapter 26

His phone chirped.

'I need you come now bring your keys am in the bedroom.'

"What the fuck?"

"Who is it?" Andy drawled from the other end of the sofa as he lay staring at the TV. The screen showed a New York street with several police cars exploding.

"It's Soph, she says 'I need you come now bring your keys am in the bedroom.' What the hell does that mean? She could be struggling with a heavy box, she could be ill or in trouble."

Andy sat up.

"You better get over there mate, I'll call you a cab."

"Ok. Shit what if it's happening again, what if she's bleeding? I can't go through that again." He choked back a sob.

"Text her, tell her you're on your way but ask if she's ok."

"Good idea." Andy was already ordering the taxi on his mobile.

'Am leaving now r u ok?'

'Just need to c u dnt worry am ok.'

"She says she's ok."

"Thank fuck for that. The cab's on its way, it'll meet you outside. Text me ok?"

"Ok, thanks mate."

* * *

The house was completely dark as he opened the door and switched off the alarm.

"SOPH...SOPH?"

"Up here."

162

Her voice sounded fine, a little croaky but ok, not scared. Despite his fear he took the stairs two at a time and as he pushed the bedroom door open he let out a huge breath, completely unaware that he'd been holding it.

She was lying in bed covered by a sheet, her shape barely distinguishable. The bed was disheveled and her hair was seriously mussed. She looked as if she'd just had sex.

"You ok?"

"Come here. I need you."

He approached the bed and sat down next to her.

"Sophie, what's wrong, has someone been here? Are you hurt?"

Sitting up she reached to put her hands around his neck.

"No, numb-nuts. I'm just horny and I had a wet dream about you."

"Really?" He started to grin.

"Yes really, so get over your ego and sort it."

"Surely not?... In your condition?... Really? Are you allowed?"

As a huge laugh burst from her she grinned.

"Am I allowed? What are you like? Of course I'm allowed."

"Soph I don't think I can really. I'm sorry it's just that after what happened before I'm scared you'll lose the baby. Sorry sweetheart, I really want you and I'm so hard it's killing me but I don't think I dare." He stood to go and she struggled to get up from the bed.

"Wait, Tom please stay, for bit at least. Please."

He turned and as she got to her feet he took in her new body. The large breasts, dark nipples, swollen belly, the brown line of the linea nigra and he was rooted to the spot.

Grabbing the sheet to cover herself he saw her blush. "Just go will you," as her voice broke she turned away.

"You must be joking." He walked towards her and taking her shoulders turned her to face him. "Drop the sheet."

"Please, Tom don't look at me, I look huge."

"Sophie, drop the sheet!"

With just a soft sigh the fabric fell to the floor and he followed it onto his knees before her.

He laid his head against her stomach and grabbed her buttocks.

"You've never looked more beautiful or more sexy," he sighed.

"Bullshit."

He looked up at her and she saw tears in his eyes.

"Let's lie down and see what happens eh? I just have to text Andy first ok?"

"You're joking right? Is there something I should know?"

"He was just worried about you that's all."

"Aw that's so sweet, bless him," she smiled warmly.

Within seconds he had put down his phone and was leading her to the bed. He helped her settle and lay down beside her.

Unable to take his eyes off her body he began to stroke her shoulders, breasts, and belly. She wriggled down the bed and moaned apprecia-tively as she spread her thighs.

"Touch me. Please, Tom."

Moving to kneel between her thighs he parted her lips with his hands and as he opened her she gasped. "You are gorgeous," he said grin-ning at her.

He reached for a nipple and was amazed at how large it had become as he pinched and tweaked it.

She moved his other hand on to her clitoris. "Please, Tom I need this."

He smiled as he began stroking her growing nub. She closed her eyes and let out a low moan. Slowly he leant down and took her nub in his mouth and softly sucked. As if an electric shock had gone through her body she bucked off the mattress and gripped the sheets with both fists.

"Oh my God," she panted.

He felt the moisture on his face and reveled in the taste of her juice. Sliding his tongue into her he felt her squeeze down on him as her climax approached.

"I want you inside me, Tom please...now."

"Are you sure?... Is it safe?"

"If you don't fuck me I think I'll spontaneously combust. Dear God...I can't bear this... PLEASE." Her hips were thrusting off the mattress as she shuddered towards her orgasm. He was certainly ready; in fact he was so hard he ached. He looked at her breasts as her body convulsed and knew he wanted her as much as she yearned for him.

Moving to lay at a right angle to her, he turned on his side and slipped her thighs over his hips and eased himself inside her. She was soaked and so very, very hot. He gasped as the sensation of her surrounded him. He reached down to stroke her engorged clitoris as they both came.

For several minutes they lay silently, both catching their breath.

"I don't know what to say," he whispered. "That was absolutely amazing."

"Yes, it was, I really needed that. Thanks."

He laughed. "No, thank you. Oh, Soph I've missed you so much I'm so glad you text me tonight."

"Well I always said that if I had an itch you were always the man to scratch it. Do you want to use the loo first or shall I?"

She pulled away from him and eased herself up on to her elbows.

"Actually, I'd rather just snuggle up with you if that's ok?"

Smiling she started shaking her head. "Oh, Tom you're so naïve. This isn't some romantic reunion; it was as you said in the past 'just sex it didn't mean anything'."

"What?"

"I needed a shag, that's all. I was feeling horny. I tried the rabbit, I tried to finger my-self but I just ended up frustrated, can't quite reach these days that's the trouble. Please set the alarm and lock up when you go."

She rolled onto her side and pushed herself up to standing.

"If this is payback, I get it. It's ok, I deserve everything you throw at me, I'll take it and I won't complain. Just seeing you and being in-volved in your life and the baby's life is enough."

"Whatever, just see yourself out will you, I'm gonna shower." She headed for the bathroom and shut the door behind her. As he gathered his clothes and started to dress he heard the shower start. He was overwhelmed by sadness and desperately wanted to take her in his arms and hold her all night but he knew he'd lost that right a long time ago.

* * *

Holding a towel against her face to muffle her sobs she leant against the closed door. The shower was running and she was sure he couldn't hear her but she wasn't prepared to take the risk. She still felt the heat between her legs as their combined juices slid from inside her. She was sexually satisfied but emotionally empty. She'd longed to hold him, to kiss him, to ask him to stay but she just couldn't bridge the gap inside her. She couldn't allow herself to be that vulnerable again. He was a rapist, a cheat and a womanizer and she wasn't prepared to be hurt by him again.

* * *

In silence he descended the stairs, reset the alarm and let himself out. He could feel her on his cock, smell her on his fingers and face and see her in his mind. She was stunning, more desirable than he'd ever imagined, wetter, hotter, sexier. He felt himself growing hard again. He longed to go back up the stairs, force the bathroom door open, take her in his arms and insist that he stay the night but the memory of the last time he'd forced himself on her thrust out of the dark crevice in his mind and burst into his consciousness. His breath caught in his chest. He saw her vulnerability and realized just how much she'd risked to allow him into her bed. He would have to wait.

CHAPTER 27

Her mobile chirped.

'I have yr stuff shal I pop it over?'

'Ok.'

Without realizing she made her way to the hall mirror and checked her hair and make-up. Deciding she looked ok she sat down in the lounge with her swollen feet on the footstool.

'Use yr key,' she text.

Against her better judgment she felt that all too familiar flutter of excitement and arousal.

Eventually she heard the door open and she tried unsuccessfully to calm herself. In response her bump woke up and started doing somersaults.

"Soph?"

"In here, quick. Come and see this."

Dropping the carrier bags he ran to the lounge to see that her hand was resting on her stomach and it was moving vigorously.

"Oh my God, that's incredible. Is that all her doing that?"

"Yep, want to feel?"

He beamed. "Hell yeh. If that's ok?"

She took his hand and placed it on her stomach. Instantly the surface of her belly began to undulate and move. His eyes filled with tears as he struggled to find the words to deal with the experience.

"It's cool isn't it? She's so strong."

"I knew babies kicked but I had no idea it was so ferocious. Does it hurt?"

She smiled. "It's a little uncomfortable sometimes but it doesn't hurt. She must have heard you come in." Addressing her comments to her belly she cooed, "hey baby, it's your daddy, are you saying hello?"

Overwhelmed Tom pushed himself up and left the room, wiping his eyes.

"TOM TOM, I'm sorry...come back please."

His head appeared around the door jamb and she smiled reassuringly.

"Sorry about that I just got a bit emotional about what you said."

Reaching for his hand she took it and placed it back on her bump.

"Well daddy you've got seven and a half months to make up for and if you're serious about being involved this is an excellent start. She can hear your voice and get used to you so why don't you introduce yourself?"

Staring at her he was unsure whether she was teasing him or if she was serious.

"Really?"

"Go on numb-nuts," she giggled.

Without breaking eye contact with her he gently lifted her top and placed his ear against her bare stomach.

"Hello sweetheart, it's daddy, I'm so sorry I haven't been around for you and mummy so far. I was a total dick and mummy quite rightly wanted to make sure I was up to being your dad before she let me speak to you," he saw her eyes filling up. "You look so beautiful in your scan pictures I can't wait to meet you, I love you baby Wilkes," and as he kissed her bump the tears ran down her face.

"You're right," she giggled. "You are a total dick."

"I know. Let me show you what I've bought."

Re-covering her stomach she followed him into the kitchen as he emptied the carriers onto the table. Everything from her list spilled out.

"Tom, thank you so much, that's brilliant."

"I told you I'd get whatever you needed."

"Yes but I thought you'd probably balk at this lot. Were you embarrassed?"

"Only a bit, the shop assistant was very helpful. I just told her what you'd written and she showed me where it all was."

"Even got sanitary towels and nipple shields, well done. I'm impressed, especially as you could have bought this all on-line."

"What? Oh shit I didn't think of that, bollocks." They both burst out laughing.

"You cock," she teased.

"I did buy something that wasn't on the list."

"Oh yeh what?"

He drew a small carrier from behind his leg.

"Just this."

She opened the bag and withdrew a white sleep suit embroidered with tiny, pink flowers and the words 'daddies' girl'.

"Oh, Tom that's so gorgeous, thanks."

"Why are you thanking me, it's the dad's job to buy nice things for his little girl. It says in the handbook, anyway I felt a bit bad not buying her anything. What else does she need? There must be loads of things to buy."

Reaching out her hand she said, "come with me."

She led him up the stairs and opened the door to the second bedroom. Too stunned to move he stood in the doorway and scanned the room.

The walls were delicate soft lavender with a matching border of pink and purple teddies. A white cot sat in the middle of the room dressed with matching linen and mobile. A white changing unit was against the wall next to a matching wardrobe. Opposite sat a white rocker with lavender cushions. The shelves were stacked with baby-wipes, muslins, cotton-wool and baby toiletries. A large pack of nappies stood on the floor.

"Open the wardrobe," she instructed.

He took in the rows of tiny baby-gros, sleep suits, cardigans and dresses. The drawers were full of vests, bibs and socks.

"You see, I asked for those things for me because she has everything she needs. The buggy and car-seat are in the cupboard under the stairs. It was me, I didn't have anything to use after I have her. I wasn't being a cow or trying to embarrass you."

"You amaze me, what you've done. It's incredible. All on your own." His voice caught with emotion. "You blow me away you know that, I don't know what to say, except I'm sorry that you've had to do this alone, I really am but you've done an amazing job."

"With respect I had to because if I'd waited for you she'd be coming home to sleep in a drawer."

"That's a little unfair, I didn't know she existed otherwise I'd have paid for all of this."

"Well technically you'd have to have paid for all of this for your other baby as well so you probably wouldn't have been able to afford to do both and I guess your *girlfriend* doesn't have a job."

"Let's not do this shall we?"

"Ooh did I hit a nerve?"

"I don't want to have this conversation."

"You started it, well your dick did."

Turning to leave the room he leant in to kiss her cheek and hug her.

"Thank you so much for earlier and for the scan pictures. It was incredible. I'm not going to argue with you anymore. You're the mother of my child and I'm gonna take care of you both whether you like it or not."

* * *

Opening the front door he grinned. Mike was standing on the doorstep with two enormous suitcases. Falling into each other's arms they kissed deeply.

"God I have really missed you."

"Me too, come in; let me help you with the cases."

"You look gorgeous. I'm hard already and you've only just walked in the door."

Placing his hand over Andy's flies Mike squeezed appreciatively.

"Drink or bed?"

"Oh bed definitely I think."

They both grinned as they linked hands and walked into the bedroom. Settling himself on the bed Andy leant back to watch.

"Undress for me. Slowly."

"Ok."

Barely able to control his lust Mike began un-buttoning his shirt. As he dropped the garment to the floor Andy smiled. "Who's been working out?"

Mike smiled back. Very slowly he undid his belt and pulled it through the loops of his jeans. Without breaking eye contact he kicked off his trainers and began to undo his button fly. As the fabric parted his erection pushed forward free-ing itself. Andy licked his lips. The jeans slid to the floor and Mike stepped away.

"Come here," Andy growled and as Mike ap-proached he leant and took the throbbing shaft into his mouth. Mike's head fell back as he moaned. As Andy worked his mouth Mike reached down and stopped him. Without removing his mouth he looked up at Mike and frowned.

"I want to look at you, touch you, come inside you."

Silently they swapped places and as Andy slowly removed each garment Mike worked his cock and smiled.

Standing naked and fully hard in front of the bed Andy took his penis in his hand and began to massage himself. With their eyes still locked he reached over to the bedside table and brought out a tube of playgel and a condom.

"I want you."

CHAPTER 28

"Sophie Wilkes."

"Ok," she called out as the midwife's head disappeared back into the treatment room.

"Here let me help you, these chairs are way too low for pregnant women, I'm gonna complain."

Offering her a hand, he pulled her up.

"Shush you. If I'm not complaining neither are you ok?"

Putting his hands up in submission he grinned.

"Ok, ok, whatever."

"Hi, Sophie how's things? Hello is this Mr Wilkes?"

As they both sat Sophie introduced Tom. "Tom's been working away but he's back and he'll be here for the birth."

"That's great news; I'm so pleased for you both."

The young, blonde, midwife beamed appreciatively. Taking in the navy blue uniform for one nanosecond Tom imagined a bedbath scenario and desperately pushed it to the back of his mind.

Producing a urine sample Sophie seemed quite at ease with the check-up but Tom had no idea what to expect. His imagination had his wife half naked, legs akimbo up in stirrups with the sexy midwife caressing her until they both came and invited him to join in. It occurred to him that perhaps he should watch a little less porn.

The midwife took the sample and tested it with a white stick and proclaimed it 'fine'. Next she took Sophie's blood pressure which likewise was acceptable. Lastly she helped Sophie onto the examination couch and he felt his cock stir and his face redden. As her belly was exposed he beamed and was instantly absorbed by the sight. The midwife pushed the bump around and seemed to jiggle it around low down by Sophie's pelvis. Her knickers stayed on and he was extremely grateful, because for some strange reason the kinky threesome he'd been imagining suddenly seemed completely inappropriate and crude with the mother of his child.

"She's head down but not engaged yet. Is she still quite active?"

"I should say so," Sophie glanced at Tom and he grinned, nodding.

"Right, so you've got about five and a half weeks left then? Let's just check the fetal heart."

Producing a small hand held ultrasound machine the midwife rubbed it over Sophie's belly until she picked up a sound like a small steam engine. Both women smiled but Tom was speechless.

"Is that it? Is that her heartbeat?"

"Haven't you heard it before, Tom?"

"No I've not been able to come to any appointments."

"That's your babies' heartbeat. Nice and strong."

He moved across the room to take Sophie's hand.

"That's amazing; I can't believe that...I'm totally blown away."

Sophie struggled to sit up and the midwife reached to help her but Tom got there first. Treating her like fine china he eased her to the edge of the couch and helped her stand.

"She can't come soon enough if you ask me. I'm really uncomfortable now, it's hard to sit, stand, even lay down. Thank God I finish work in ten days."

"Ok then I'll see you in a week's time. Get plenty of rest, I'm trusting Tom to take care of you."

"Of course I will." He smiled as he reached to take her hand.

Once outside the surgery she pulled away.

"Thanks for coming but you really don't need to play the dutiful husband you know."

"That's not why I held your hand. I did it because I wanted to."

"Mmm well I don't want to hold your hand so please don't touch me like that again."

"Except when you're horny late at night then?" Turning to leave she scowled.

"Piss off, Tom."

"Don't you mean 'fuck me Tom'?"

"Why are you doing this? Why are you pushing me like this? It was sex, just sex; you're here because of the baby not because of me. We have nothing. An occasional fuck doesn't make a marriage."

Putting his hands on her shoulders he turned her to face him.

"I have been a total bastard. I get that, I went completely off the rails but if you think that there wasn't a spark between us the other night you're a liar, if you think I'm not gonna keep trying to get you back every chance I get you're a fool. I've always loved you, I loved you when I cheated, I loved you when I left, I love you now. I just couldn't see what I had in front of me. I was a total arsehole but I'm not going anywhere so you better get used to this," and he bent to kiss her hard on the mouth and as his tongue sought hers her body responded.

* * *

Andy eased away from Mike and discarded the condom. Both were bathed in sweat and were flushed and grinning.

"That was worth every second of that hellish flight."

"Tell me about it. Bloody hell, you're gorgeous."

They kissed.

Mike stood and went into the kitchen returning a few minutes later with two glasses of JD.

"Cheers."

"I have something to say and you might need a drink."

"Oh shit. What the fuck...is it bad news? Has something happened? Are you ok?"

"Relax, relax, I'm fine. It's just something I have to say and I flew all the way from New York to say it so here we go."

Andy took his hand reassuringly.

"Ok, go on then."

Mike took a deep breath and reached to cover his groin with the sheet. The symbolism of the subconscious gesture wasn't lost on Andy.

"Andy, I love you, in fact I'm in love with you."

Andy opened his mouth to interrupt.

"No, please let me finish. I know you don't love me but I don't care. I wanna be with you regardless. I want us to live together and try to make it work. I'm not Tom but he's never gonna be with you, it's just not gonna happen and you know it. We can make this work I know we can. Please give this some serious thought. That's it."

He slumped back against the headboard. Andy reached out and stroked Mike's cheek.

"You blow me away, you really do. I'm so flattered."

Mike stood up, pushing Andy away and hurried to the patio doors, threw them open and stepped out into the cool autumn evening, hugging the sheet around him.

"'You're flattered', even I know that's not good. Look I'll get dressed and be out of here before you know it." A sob caught in his throat.

"Like hell you will." Andy flew onto the balcony and his arms went round Mike's waist as he laid his head between his lover's shoulder blades.

"Just shut up and let me finish dick-head." Mike smirked as he continued.

"I have missed you so much. You're the one person I actually thought I could be with for the rest of my life. Our time in New York was incredible. I've never been so happy. I gave up on Tom along time ago. It's ok, I will always love him but I'm not *in love* with him anymore. What you just said took my breath away. I would love to live with you."

Mike spun round.

"What? Really?"

"Yes really, you and me together, a proper couple, you know, faithful, monogamous, all that serious relationship shit, IKEA, garden centers. All that domestic stuff."

Mike's mouth found Andy's and as they kissed Mike's tears fell.

* * *

"I've been thinking."

"Easy."

"I'm moving back in."

Sophie's head spun round.

"Hang on a minute; you can't just decide to move back in."

"Actually I can, but just let me finish. It's Halloween tomorrow which means you'll be up and down to the door all evening and with bonfire night around the corner I want to make sure you're safe and getting your rest. I don't want you struggling to put bins out in the dark or worrying about getting milk and bread now the clocks have changed. Apart from that you only have a couple of weeks left and if she comes early I want to make sure I'm here and FYI this is non-negotiable."

She rubbed her belly thoughtfully.

"Well, you're here every evening so what the hell, go for it, just one question. Where are you gonna sleep?"

"That's up to you; I can sleep in the spare room if you like?"

As she struggled to stand he reached out to pull her to her feet.

"I'm not taking you back, Tom you're here to help with the baby that's all."

"So I'll only be making the trip across the landing if you feel horny then?" He asked her grinning.

"You bastard," she teased. "That's not fair, it's just my hormones."

"If it makes you feel better to think that go ahead, but quite frankly, you're back to being a totally dirty, horny, bitch and I love it."

"Do you?"

"Fucking hell, Soph are you kidding? You look so sexy I could shag you five ways from Sunday and still be hard. You know what you want and when and that's always turned me on about you."

"Yeh right, unless it was a baby huh? Not so much of a turn on then eh?"

He put his index finger on her lips.

"We can't go on like this, we both said and did things we shouldn't, I'm not gonna discuss it anymore. I've apologized over and over and now it's done and put away." Placing his hand on her belly he looked her in the eye. "For her sake as well as our sanity. No more."

Walking past him she brushed against him and let his hand touch her buttock.

"When are you moving in then?"

He followed her into the kitchen. "I thought tomorrow, it's Saturday and I'm off work."

"Ok, that's fine."

"I'll put my stuff wherever you like ok?"

Leaning against the worktop she sighed.

"What?"

"Well, I never imagined I'd have you in this house again let alone let you move back. I'm mad." He took her face in his hands and kissed her deeply.

"I'm glad you have."

She pushed her breasts against his chest and let her hand find his erection through his jeans.

They kissed again and his hand moved down her back to grasp her buttock.

"Come with me."

"What?"

"Come with me." Taking her hand he led her into the lounge and eased her towards the recliner.

"Hang on a minute."

After cranking up the heating he began to re-move her clothes, kissing every bit of exposed flesh as he went until she was naked and breath-less, he then eased her down into the chair and leant it back until it she lay before him, fully exposed.

Sitting beside her on the floor he eased her legs apart and began to stroke the inside of her thighs.

"Ooh that's nice."

"Good," he whispered.

As his fingers worked higher he began to stroke her soft downy pubes and tease her lips apart. Opening her thighs widely now her breath started to come in gasps.

"You're so beautiful."

As he bent her knees up he gazed at her wet opening and carefully traced the shape of each fold. As he grazed her clitoris she bucked off the chair.

"God, you're so wet."

"Finger me, please."

As he slid two fingers into her hot depths she bore down on his hand and he almost came in his pants.

She ran her hands over her breasts and teased her nipples until he pushed her hands away and took one in his mouth as his hand worked the other.

"Ooh, more I want more. Open me up, stretch me open. Please."

Meeting her eyes he frowned. "Are you sure? I might hurt you."

"Tom I need this it will help with the birth and I'd rather you do it than some doctor or mid-wife. I'm wet and horny, now's the perfect time. Please, you won't hurt me and if I want you to stop I'll tell you. I promise."

Gently and against his better judgment he eased a third finger into her and felt her sigh. Working his fingers back and forth he felt her relax. Eventually he tried a fourth and although she felt tight he found as she relaxed her body eased to accommodate him.

"That's nice. That feels really good."

"You sure?"

"Abso-fucking-lutely," she grinned.

As he pushed his hand further into her she reached down and held his wrist.

"Hang on. I think that's enough."

Struggling to pull his fingers out he looked terrified.

"Hey don't stop, just don't go any further that's all."

"Am I hurting you?"

"No and that's how I want it to stay. Is that all four?"

"Yep, all the way to the knuckle."

"Feels nice, just move your hand in and out slowly."

Moving as she instructed he watched as her face changed and her body spasmed into orgasm driving herself onto his hand.

As her climax subsided she opened her eyes to see him smiling at her.

"Let's lay on the rug."

"Are you sure you'll be comfortable there?"

"Just give me a hand will you."

"I thought I just had."

"Very funny."

As he helped her onto all fours and onto the floor he watched as she lay down.

"Undress for me," she whispered.

He slowly removed his clothes and as he freed his cock he looked down to see her stroking herself.

"Jeez, you're so sexy."

Kneeling between her thighs he took over from her and bent to take her clitoris in his mouth. Again he felt her orgasm nearing and as he sucked on the hard little nub she began to rock her hips.

"I want us to come with you inside me," she breathed as she rolled onto her side. Lying down behind her he eased into her and they both gasped at the sensation. Unable to move for fear of coming he lay still and felt her pussy sucking at him. He held on to her as she came and as she quieted he began to slide in and out of her so very slowly, almost pulling out with each stroke and then opening her up with each re-entry. The sensation was indescribable. He felt her coming again and as he finally let go they came together.

CHAPTER 29

"And', I'm gonna need that stuff dropping over to the house today is that ok? I've hired the van."

"That's fine mate. No worries."

"I'm gonna move my clothes back in this morning and then I'm taking Soph to her baby shower. While she's with her mates I can put the house back together and surprise her."

"Sounds like a plan. Mike said he can give us a hand."

"Cool. See you about half two."

He rested against the worktop as the kettle boiled and grinned. By the time he picked her up this afternoon their stuff would be back in the house, all the items she'd had to sell would be there waiting.

* * *

"Shit, it's gone straight to voicemail. Tom, hi it's Sam, I work with Sophie, erm, there's a bit of a problem. I'm on my way to St Georges with Soph, her waters have broken and she's having regular contractions. Ring me when you get this or better still get to the hospital."

* * *

Tom placed the signed Chelsea shirt back on the wall and grinned. "That's it, the last bit done. Thanks guys. I owe you a few rounds for all this."

"No worries mate, she's gonna be so surprised."

"Looks like home now, love it. Have you seen my mobile?"

Mike frowned, "I think I saw it in the van when we arrived."

"Better check what time she needs picking up."

Walking out to the hired van he saw his phone on the dash and noticed his missed call and voicemail icons were flashing.

"Typical."

As he listened to his voicemail his face dropped.

"No, no, no. Fucking hell."

Jumping into the van he pulled out into the traffic and sped towards the hospital.

* * *

Sitting at the kitchen table she stared at the red spot on the page. She counted the days. Six. Six days late.

Alex's head appeared over her shoulder.

"Wotcha doing?"

"Nothing."

"Bullshit. You're checking the dates."

"No I'm not."

"Yes you are. I know you didn't come on."

Standing up to grab him she buried her face in his chest.

"It's ok. Either way it's ok," he reassured her as he stroked her hair.

She mumbled into the fabric.

"Hey, come out of there I can't hear you."

Lifting her head she smiled.

"Stupid boy. I said I'm just so scared."

"I know, me too. Do you want to do a test?"

"I don't know."

"Isn't it better to know?"

"Yes, no, maybe. Oh shit I don't know. You decide."

"Ok, come on then, upstairs. Do you need a drink or can you squeeze one out for the team?"

She hesitated.

"I think I can squeeze the lemon."

"Come on then. Do you want me to come in with you whilst you wait?"

"Please. Sure you don't mind?"

"Jesus woman, when was the last time we closed the bathroom door in this house? I'm sure if I can see you pissing every other day I can sure see you pissing today."

Taking her hand he led her up the stairs to the bathroom and took the test from the cabinet.

"Go on then, do your stuff."

Dropping her jeans and pants she passed the stick through the stream of urine.

Chapter 30

"Sophie Wilkes, which room please?"

"Room seven. Are you family?"

"I'm her husband."

"Go right in, Mr Wilkes. Down the corridor, it's the fourth on the right."

Taking the corridor at a run he reached the room and as he opened the door he noticed his hand was shaking.

She was dressed in a hospital gown, sitting on a stool with her arms folded on the bed and her head on her arms moaning softly as the woman rubbed her back.

"Tom?"

Her voice broke as he hurried to her and kissed her sweaty forehead. The woman cleared her throat.

"Hi, I'm Sam. I'm so glad you got my message."

"Hi, I'm really sorry I didn't take the call. I lost my phone temporarily."

"Don't worry you're here now, I'll step outside and leave you two alone for a bit."

"Thanks."

"How you doing babe?"

She began to pant and grimace as a contraction swept over her.

"Ooh that was a big one." She looked at the clock, "two minutes apart now."

His eyes filled with tears as he rubbed her back and kissed her hair.

"It's my fault isn't it? She's coming too soon just 'cause I couldn't keep my fucking dick to myself. I am so, so, sorry."

"Shut up will you. She's not coming too soon, she's just a few days early and sex is good for getting things going. It's not your fault tit-head."

He smiled. "You say the sweetest things."

She play punched his arm as another contraction arrived.

"Oooowwww SHIT!"

This one seemed more ferocious he noted and it certainly hadn't been two minutes since the last one.

As the pain abated he brushed the hair from her face.

"Shouldn't someone be here with you, like a doctor or nurse or something?"

"The midwife comes in every half an hour and I can ring if I need her."

"What about an epidural or something for the pain?" Her eyes closed as another wave hit her.

"OOOOWWWW! FUCK THAT HURTS. TOM RING THE BELL."

She gripped the sheet until her knuckles turned white and threw her head back and groaned as he pressed the call bell.

* * *

"Er...And'."

"Yeh."

"The van's gone."

"What do you mean gone?"

"It's gone as in not there and incidentally, so's Tom."

"What the hell is he doing? I'll ring him."

* * *

"Hi, Sophie how you doing?"

"She's in fucking agony and nobody seems to give a damn, will you stop asking stupid questions and help her. Please." The midwife smiled reassuringly.

"Sorry you're having a rough time; I'm here now so let's take a look at you shall we?"

Helping Sophie onto the bed he heard his phone ring.

"Bollocks."

"Tom, why don't you step outside for a minute whilst I see how Sophie's doing?"

"Hell no."

Raising her hands in submission she nodded.

"Ok, no problem."

As she approached Sophie another ferocious contraction rocked her.

"That looked like a big one."

Tom opened his mouth to speak but instead Sophie nodded as she placed a hand on his arm.

"Ok, let's check you before the next one arrives."

He helped Sophie raise her knees as the midwife slid two fingers into her. Sophie grimaced as the woman moved her arm around and pushed into her.

Eventually she withdrew as another contraction crashed over her.

Sophie screamed as she threw her head back and gasped.

"Sophie, look at me. You're almost fully dilated and you'll want to push in the next hour or so. I think you need some pain relief, let's get you some pethadine and some gas and air ok?"

"Thank God for that," he mumbled.

Placing the mouth piece between Sophie's lips she showed them both how it worked and left to get the injection.

The contractions were coming about forty seconds apart now and there was no time for Sophie to recover and as each one hit her she screamed. The gas and air helped focus her attention and take the edge off the pain but it broke his heart to see her so distressed.

Several minutes later two midwives came in with the pethadine and having checked her wrist band they gave the injection.

The midwives stayed with her as each contraction, stronger than the last washed over her until there seemed no break between them.

Between the three of them they rubbed her back, gave her sips of water, wiped her forehead, and whispered encouragement. Sometime during labor her gown had slipped away and she lay naked, sweaty, disorientated, but seemingly focused on her goal.

"I want to push," she whispered.

"What sweetheart? What did you say?"

"I SAID I WANT TO PUSH AND I'M NOT YOUR SWEETHEART YOU CHEATING BASTARD."

"What the fuck?" He staggered away from the bed as Sophie bellowed at him.

"Tom it's ok, it's part of this stage of labor, she doesn't mean it."

"LIKE FUCK I DON'T."

"Ok, Sophie let's see how you're doing I think you're nearly there. When you want to push I need you to pant for me ok? Tom and I will help you; pant not push, just while we see if you're fully dilated ok?"

Sophie nodded as her face twisted in pain.

"Look at me babe, now pant...like this...that's it..."

Without breaking eye contact they panted together through the waves of pain and the urge to bear down.

Removing her fingers the midwife smiled.

"Ok my love, here we go. I want you to push into your bottom. The next time you feel the urge to bear down just go with it."

"Ok that's it. I can see the head."

"AAAHHH."

"That's it sweetheart. Keep pushing you're almost there."

Sophie was on all fours and as she pushed she vaguely heard one of the midwives call him to see the head coming out.

"I can see her babe, she's almost here." His voice seemed a million miles away. She felt the overwhelming urge to bear down and the dreadful tearing and burning inside her.

"That's it now, keep going you're doing really well, the head's out, Sophie one last push."

And as she pushed she felt the warm, slippery slither as her daughter's body slipped from her.

"She's not crying. SHE'S NOT CRYING. WHAT'S GOING ON?" she screamed.

CHAPTER 31

"Let's have a look."
  "I don't want to."
  "Well I do."
He took the plastic wand and scrutinized it, frowning.
  "Well?"
  "You said you didn't want to know."
  "Just fucking tell me will you?"
  "Ok mummy, are you sure you want to know."
  "Did you just say mummy?"
  "That's what they call pregnant women isn't it?"
She threw her arms around his neck and kissed him hard on the mouth.
  "I love you so much."
  "I love you so much too."

* * *

The midwives worked on the silent bundle as Sophie and Tom wept, clinging to each other.
  Eventually a small whimper escaped followed by a huge cry.
  "Here you are. She's fine just a bit of fluid needed sucking out before she could get her breath."
The small, pink, wrinkled bundle instantly quietened as Sophie took her in her arms and placed her to the breast, murmuring reassuringly. As Sophie fed their daughter Tom noticed the cord was still attached to her at one end and disappeared between Sophie's legs. Gesturing towards it Tom cleared his throat.
  "Shouldn't that be cut off or something?"

"Now she's breathing yes. We left it so she was still, able to get oxygen from her mum until, she could breathe by herself."

"That makes sense. God I'm so glad you two were here. Sorry I've been so stroppy."

Both midwives smiled.

"Would you like to cut the cord?"

"Hell yeh."

"Come on then. I'll talk you through it, you can't hurt either of them so don't be afraid."

As one midwife administered the injection and delivered the afterbirth the other took the baby, weighed and checked her and put a tiny band on her little wrist before handing her back.

"She's 3290 grams, that's seven pounds four ounces in real money. You have a tiny tear but you'll only need a couple of stitches."

"Tom, can you make some phone calls whilst they stitch me up."

"I don't want to leave either of you."

"Please just let mum and dad know at least."

"Ok." He kissed her gently on the mouth and brushed his daughter's forehead with his lips.

"Er,…Soph…what's her name?"

She laughed, "I can't believe you waited all this time to ask me. It's Hope."

Too choked to speak he turned away to hide his tears.

* * *

"Where the fuck are you? It's nearly midnight?"

"It's a girl, seven pounds four ounces, called Hope."

"What the fuck are you on about? We've been worried sick, you just disappeared...hang on...a girl...did you have the baby?"

"Oh my God yeh. I found my phone and there was a voicemail saying Soph was in labor."

"Shit mate...congratulations."

"Thanks, it was so awful and so wonderful I can't tell you, she didn't cry straight away and we were both crying, then she bellowed and it was the best feeling."

"Hi, Tom its Mike."

"Hi mate."

"Congratulations, I'm afraid Andy's too choked up to speak, he's crying his eyes out actually."

"Give him a hug from me; I'll talk to him later ok?"

"Will do. Love to Sophie and the baby."

"Before you go mate can you guys do me a favor, can you get the two overnight bags out of the nursery and the car seat from under the stairs, put them in my car and bring it to the hospital car-park. Text me when you get there and I'll come out and meet you and you can pick up the van. Is that ok?"

"Course, no worries, see you in a bit."

"Cheers."

* * *

He had never driven so carefully or so slowly.

"Tom, get a bloody move on will you. She'll be starting school before we get home."

"Very funny."

Hope snuffled.

"Is she ok? Should I stop?"

He craned his neck desperate to see the car seat in the rear-view mirror.

"She's fine but she says, for Christ's sake hurry up dad, I'm starving."

"Everyone's a bloody comedian."

Sophie giggled as she stroked Hope's tiny forehead.

"Seriously, Tom I'm getting soaked here please get us home before we're awash in the back."

"Ok, ok. What time did you say your parent's flight gets in?"

"They said about ten thirty tomorrow morning."

"Am I picking them up?"

"No I said they should make their own way. I want you here with us."

Catching her eye in the mirror they both smiled.

As he pulled up outside the house and opened the back door he noticed her shirt and gasped.

"Shit, Soph you're soaked."

"I know, it's ok, it's quite normal until she starts taking a bit more, then I'll adjust to her demands and produce less. Feels disgusting though I have to say. Cold and sticky."

"Er babe, you look like you just won first place in a wet t-shirt contest and I'm getting a hard-on."

She slapped him on the arm. "Dream on mate, this is now a working vagina and after what it's just been through it needs six weeks off, you better warm your hand up."

"Gee thanks," he replied as he bent into kiss her.

As she opened the front door she stood back to allow him to enter first with the car seat. He walked into the kitchen and placing Hope's seat on the table turned to put the kettle on.

"TOM, come here a minute please," she called.

He followed her voice to the lounge where she stood staring at the Banksy print on the chimney breast.

"What?... How?... What's been going on? Is that my print? Are those all our CDs and DVDs by any chance?"

He grinned sheepishly.

"Actually, it's everything you sold; me and Andy bought it all."

"That's impossible. I mailed that stuff all over the place."

"I know we had to drive all over to collect it. Andy's had it at his place since then."

"You mean you actually replaced it all, everything? How did you know I'd sold some stuff?"

"I let myself in the day you told me you were pregnant, I drove straight here when you weren't home I let myself in and saw what you were up to, so then I simply bought all the stuff you were selling under different names. Andy used friend's addresses and there you go. I knew you'd sold it all to buy baby stuff, that's the only way you could have afforded it. I felt so guilty that you had to sell your belongings 'cause you were hard up that I wanted to do it, to make it up to you."

"That's why you actually paid top price for everything? I just thought I'd been lucky."

A squawk erupted from the kitchen and they both rushed to release Hope from her harness.

As Sophie settled in the recliner with Hope on a pillow, a pint of squash to hand and several muslins close by she started to feed her daughter.

She murmured soothingly as both worked to get Hope's tiny mouth latched on. As the struggle went on Hope got hungrier and noisier and Sophie got more distressed.

"I can't do it, I can't do it, she won't take it properly. Just take her will you."

Rushing to kneel beside her he put a reassuring hand over hers and took her chin in his other hand.

"You can do this, stop worrying. You fed her at the hospital, you're tired and stressed that's all, relax and breathe. What did the breast feeding advisor say, wait till her mouth's really open and then push her head onto the whole nipple, the surrounding bit too so she's not just sucking on the nipple."

"Ok, ok, you're right I can do this. Ok baby, here we go."

And Sophie squeezed a tiny drop of milk onto Hope's lips and as she smelt the milk she opened her mouth and Sophie guided her on. Within seconds Hope was suckling contentedly.

Tom leant to kiss Sophie's smiling face and couldn't resist catching a drop of breast milk from the other nipple and putting it to his lips.

Sophie tried to laugh without disturbing her daughter. "Ha, I knew it, I knew you wouldn't be able to resist you kinky bugger."

"What? It's natural curiosity that's all."

CHAPTER 32

"I really can't believe you did all that for me, you went to all that trouble to replace everything."

"I had to, I was so upset at the thought of you worrying about money and being hard up, especially as I was living with Andy rent-free."

"Yes but you were still paying half the mortgage here."

"If I'd have known before I would have paid for everything, for her I mean."

"I know."

As he put his arm round her shoulders she leant into him as they snuggled on the sofa.

"I really am so touched you went to so much trouble to buy it all in secret and then put it all back whilst I was out so you could surprise me. That's really very romantic."

"Sod off," he grinned. "I'm not romantic, you know that, I'm a thoughtless, sex obsessed pervert who happens to be the luckiest man in the world right about now."

"Really?"

"Yeh really. Sophie, I have to say something and I don't want you to read anything into it ok. I'm not asking to get back with you officially or anything, I just have to say this ok?"

"Ok."

"I love you, I'm in love with you, well I've fallen head over heels in love with you all over again and I'm so happy to be part of your life even though I know we're not together as it were."

She stood up and left the room.

"Bollocks."

Twenty minutes later she came back into the lounge and sat back down beside him.

"You ok?" He asked tentatively.

"Fine thanks."

"Where were you? I thought you'd freaked at what I said."

"No, I'm good."

"Erm...a little confused here, why did you walk out?"

"I needed the loo that's all."

"Christ, what have you been eating? You were gone so long I thought you'd gone on holiday."

"Tom, I've just had a baby, things are a little messed up down there. I'm sore and bleeding. I just needed a little time that's all."

"Sorry. That was really tactless of me."

"Let's go to bed."

"Soph, it's eight fifteen. Are you serious?"

She grinned up at him.

"Oh my God are you in for a shock. She'll be up in about two hours. With a newborn you sleep when you can."

"Good point. Ok then."

As she entered the master bedroom he headed for the spare room. She smiled to herself and waited for his call.

After several minutes he appeared in the doorway looking worried.

"Sophie, where's my stuff?... Are you chucking me out after what I said? Is that what you want?"

Turning to him she beckoned him over to the chest of drawers.

"Take a look. Open the drawer."

As he opened the drawer she studied his face and as it broke into a smile she reached to hug him.

"You're sleeping in here from now on and FYI I never stopped loving you. I think we lost our way and maybe fell out of love with each other but I am in love with you now and I think I always will be. Stay, Tom stay here with us, with me."

They hugged each other for several minutes neither one willing to break until eventually they became aware of the growing dampness between them and drew apart to look at the milk leaking onto their clothes. He leant down to kiss her and their tongues met.

"When did you swap my stuff over?"

"Well Sherlock, I wasn't really in the loo for twenty minutes."

"Mmm sneaky I like your style."

"Well I learnt it from you, sneaking around moving stuff."

"Point taken."

PART 5
WINTER

CHAPTER 33

His hand slid between her thighs and slowly eased them apart.

"Are you sure?" He breathed into her ear.

"Yes, it's ok, just take it slow."

"Anything you want sweetheart."

He sucked first one nipple then the other and felt each one harden in his mouth. He tasted the milk and lapped at her.

"Hey, leave some for Hope."

"Ok, that's enough then. I'd better move down a bit."

She giggled in anticipation as he traced his tongue down her stomach to her hair line. Her still slightly flabby stomach was covered in stretch marks and he kissed them lovingly.

"Open your legs, nice and wide for me I want to look at you...that's it. You are so gorgeous."

He softly stroked each glistening fold and as he ran his fingertip over her clitoris she moaned.

He'd seen her naked since the birth and he'd showered with her but he'd never actually seen her pussy since. He knew it would be different and he knew he didn't care. He just didn't want to hurt her.

Placing his face between her thighs he flicked at her with his tongue. She bucked off the mattress. He smiled. He flicked again and tasted the all too familiar wetness he craved.

"Please, don't tease me," she pleaded.

Happy to oblige he lapped at her in earnest and as he felt her shudder he rotated a finger around her tender opening. Suddenly he found a lump and instantly stopped to pull away and look at it.

"What?... Why have you stopped?"

"You have a scar, from the stitches."

"I know, what did you think would happen? Is it freaking you out? Do you want to stop?"

"Fuck no, it just makes me appreciate what you went through, does it hurt?"

"It's a little tender, but it's ok."

Reassured he swept his tongue over the scar and so very gently wriggled his tongue inside her as he began to rub her clitoris harder. He felt her hips rocking in time with his hand and as he withdrew his tongue he carefully eased a finger into her. She pushed down onto him.

"Just do it...harder...more," she gasped.

As he eased the second finger in she worked herself onto his hand and started to come ferociously.

As the climax eased she looked down her body at his smiling face.

"Lay down."

"You sure?"

"Lay down."

She mounted him and slid herself over his throbbing length. Holding her hips he steadied her, "hang on. I'll come if you move, give me a minute."

She grinned down at him, as droplets formed at her nipples and dropped onto his stomach. He was grimacing with the effort of holding back.

Before he could achieve control she moved her hips very slowly up and down his length.

"Oh fuck. I'm coming," he panted and he began shuddering towards orgasm as she rocked her hips against him.

* * *

Mothercare was heaving. The January sale had started and everyone wanted a bargain. Tom pushed the buggy around looking for some bibs while Sophie went to find some more breast pads. He heard her voice from the adjacent aisle and as he turned the corner he saw her talking to a young woman who appeared to be pregnant.

"Here they are now, Tom, this is Kirsty. We work together."

"Hi nice to meet you."

"She's expecting twins."

"Wow congratulations. That's exciting, a lot of work though."

Peering into the buggy Kirsty cooed at Hope and tickled her cheeks, evoking a smile. "Sophie she's beautiful, you must be so pleased. How are you feeling in yourself?"

"I'm fine thanks, no problems; she's good as gold and I'm still feeding her, which is great."

"How old is she now?"

"Eleven weeks, I can't believe it's gone so quickly. You here on your own or is Alex shopping with you?"

"I'm here with my sister, she's just over there. LUCY...LUCY. Come and say hello."

A young blond girl approached carrying a basket crammed with baby clothes.

Tom and Lucy's eyes met and locked.

"This is Lucy my sister. This is Sophie from work and her husband Tom and baby Hope. It was Sophie who went into labor at her baby shower. Remember I told you?"

"Hi, Lucy nice to meet you." Sophie extended a hand but Lucy's eyes were still locked on Tom's.

Kirsty nudged her sister and noticing Sophie's hand she took it and smiled.

"Your daughter is gorgeous."

"Thanks."

"She looks like your husband."

"Do you think so?"

Tom stood speechless, staring at Lucy, rooted to the spot.

Kirsty gazed at him curiously.

"Well we'd better be off; she'll be due a feed soon."

"Bye, Sophie nice to see you. Nice to meet you, Tom."

"Yeh, you too," he mumbled as he struggled to push the buggy in the opposite direction.

"I need the loo," he called as he hurried towards the Gents.

Once inside the stall he sat down and withdrew his wallet. Taking out the scan pictures he traced the tiny face and hands with his fingertip. The paper had started to become worn and frayed and he absently thought about getting it laminated but knew that was unrealistic.

A sob escaped him and he let the tears fall. When he eventually felt composed enough to meet up with Sophie her face was deeply concerned.

"Hun, are you ok?"

"No not really. I need to talk to you about something."

CHAPTER 34

Lucy's hands shook as she paid for her shopping and once outside the store she broke down.

Rushing to her Kirsty took her in her arms and held her.

"It's ok, it's ok, I understand, it's too soon. We should have waited to go baby shopping."

Lucy pushed away from her and headed for the car.

"Lucy wait."

Hurrying to catch up Kirsty reached the car as Lucy climbed in.

As she struggled to put the bags in the boot she recalled the meeting with Sophie and her husband. Her husband Tom.

"Oh shit," she whispered.

Getting into the car she reached over and took Lucy's shaking hand." That was him wasn't it?"

She just nodded.

"Fucking hell."

"Exactly."

"That must have been so hard for you."

"You think?"

"Sorry."

"He's got a baby, a three month old baby which means she was pregnant when we were together."

"Bastard."

"He must have had us both on the go."

"What a shit."

"I miss him so much."

"What the fuck...are you mad girl?"

"I love him even though he's a total bastard. I love him."

"But he treated you like shit he's not worth these tears babe. Cry for your baby not for him."

Wiping her face she nodded.

"You're right. I will cry for my son not for that shit, thanks for being there. I don't know how I got through the checkout."

"Pure will-power, just pure will-power. You're stronger than you think, trust me. You'll get through this."

"If I'm honest I have to admit I came onto him, every day, every single day, I touched his thigh and kissed him. He never encouraged me, he only ever looked that's all. I started it, it was all me. He told me he had made a mistake and that he was gonna make a go of it with his wife."

"He left her though didn't he?"

"Yes but he only left her the day I told him, which makes me wonder whether it was like a trial separation, you know to work things out?"

"You can't think like that. He slept with you, he didn't have to, he wanted to, you didn't force yourself on him. It's not your fault. He cheated on her, end of."

"I have to take responsibility though. He stood by me 'cause I was pregnant, not 'cause he really wanted me."

"Why are you doing this?"

"'Cause it's time to let him go. He's got a life with his wife and baby. I was a mistake, a fling. I know that now. He wasn't my knight in shining armor he was just vulnerable and horny and I egged him on. That's the truth."

"You're being really hard on yourself you know."

"No Kirst, I'm not, that's the truth. You all think he's a shit but I'm as much to blame as him. I knew he was married and yet I still slept with him. I got pregnant through stupidity and I paid the price. Time to put it behind me."

They hugged.

"You're amazing, I'm so proud of you."

"Oh just shut up and drive."

* * *

Sitting on opposite sides of the Starbucks table he looked into her eyes and took her hand.

"I have something to show you."

"Ok, whatever it is, it'll be ok, Tom honestly."

Letting go he reached down and placed his wallet on the table in front of them.

"I'm guessing it's not that you need a new wallet," she teased.

Smiling he shook his head "not exactly."

As he removed and unfolded the paper he stared at it before turning it to face her.

"Tom how did you get these?"

"What do you mean?"

"They're Hope's twelve week scan pictures but I only sent you the twenty week pictures."

"Look again, look at the date, the sex, the due date."

Leaning in to study the figures she slowly lifted her head and looked at him.

"Oh, Tom."

Her eyes misted and she took his hand.

"That's my son. I'm sorry about how he came to be, about the cheating but he was still my son and I loved him, even if it was only for a short time. I carry these pictures with me all the time and as far as I'm concerned I have two children and I always will. I'm sorry but that's how I feel."

Getting up she walked round to his side of the table and bent down to take him in her arms and kiss him.

"If you'd been able to dismiss your son so lightly you wouldn't be the man I love."

"Thank you, thank you. I was so scared you would freak."

"I don't like the constant reminder but I love you anyway."

"Really?"

"Yep."

CHAPTER 35

Tom came awake to the sound of his daughter stirring through the baby monitor. Sophie started to get up when he placed a hand on her arm.

"I'll go." Sleepily she smiled.

"You sure?"

"Absolutely."

Leaning over the edge of the cot they smiled into each other's eyes.

"Hello little one, wotchu doing awake? Coming downstairs with me?"

As he reached to lift her she beamed. He blew a raspberry on her neck and she giggled infectiously.

Once settled on the sofa with a warm bottle they looked into each other's eyes and it struck him how close he'd come to losing everything.

"Look at you, big girl now aren't you? God I love you so much. Of course your mum does too, we both do. Do you know how much she wanted you? She tried everything to get you. It was all she lived for. Things were bad back then, really bad, we argued a lot and I freaked out a bit. Well for about a year actually. I went off the rails. I don't expect we'll ever tell you about what really happened but I was a total shit. I lost the plot and, well you nearly had a half brother.

He died before he was born. I have a scan picture in my wallet and one day I'll show you. He was beautiful too. The weird thing is if he'd have lived I wouldn't have you and your mum back. I can't imagine that, being without you both. I guess it's just one of those, 'everything happens for a reason' situations. If I'd have known that having you would be such an incredible experience I'd have listened to your mum and tried harder. I suspect you'll find out in your own time that your mum knows best, if not about everything then about a lot. The only thing I guess I know about is what happens when people freak out and that's only 'cause it happened to me. They get pushed so hard they lash out and hurt everyone around them. They rebel and end up living a completely different life just to escape the stress. Everyone needs to feel like they have some say in their lives. I just felt like I had no control. No say and I flipped. What I really mean is that I don't ever want you to feel like you're gonna flip out and disappear into another life. No matter what happens to you, no matter how much pressure you feel I'll always be there for you. I don't ever want you to risk losing the people you love and have to live with the guilt of hurting everyone around you just 'cause you can't cope. I lost a whole year; I lost the first seven months of knowing you, of being there for your mum. The past twelve months have left a huge gap in my life and without you I'd have nothing to show for it. I feel like a storm tore through my life and now all is calm and safe but what a shit load of destruction got left in its wake. Ok, if I'm honest, and I am, I had some pretty amazing sex and that's nice to remember but in reality that doesn't really mean much. Especially as your mum is the sexiest woman on the planet and it was always better with her. I love you, Hope Wilkes. That's it, go to sleep baby."

Lightning Source UK Ltd.
Milton Keynes UK
UKOW052103110712

195835UK00001B/13/P